IRON EMPIRES
FAITH CONQUERS

COTAR • FOMAS

CHRISTOPHER MOELLER

IRON EMPIRES
FAITH CONQUERS

WRITTEN AND ILLUSTRATED BY
CHRISTOPHER MOELLER

LETTERING BY
JAMES GREER AND STEVE HAYNIE

ForgedLord
COMICS

Table of Contents

IRON EMPIRES: FAITH CONQUERS
PUBLISHED BY FORGED LORD COMICS
© 2015 CHRISTOPHER MOELLER
NEW YORK | PITTSBURGH
FLC FIRST EDITION | FIRST PRINTING
ISBN: 978-0-9836458-8-7
FORGEDLORDCOMICS.COM
MOELLERILLUSTRATIONS.COM

COTAR • FOMAS

TO FELLOW TRAVELERS
MIKE CLARK AND **NEIL ENGLEHART**

There is only
one real path—
the river of fire.

Everything else
is an illusion.

CHAPTER 1: EXILE

YEAR 597 OF THE HANRILKE ERA.

THE *BRIGHT TONG* IS ONE OF THE FASTEST SHIPS IN THE CHURCH FLEET.

FOR THE PAST YEAR SHE'S BEEN HAULING ME AT MAXIMUM DISTORTION TOWARD A STAR ON THE FROZEN RIM OF THE VOID.

VERY SOON NOW, I'LL SEE IT. AFTER A YEAR OF BLACK UNKNOWNS, I'LL FINALLY SEE PERDITION UP CLOSE.

ALRIGHT RATS! WE'LL BE OUT OF HEX IN THIRTEEN HOURS. THAT LEAVES YOU PLENTY OF TIME TO REVIEW YOUR BRIEFING FILES.

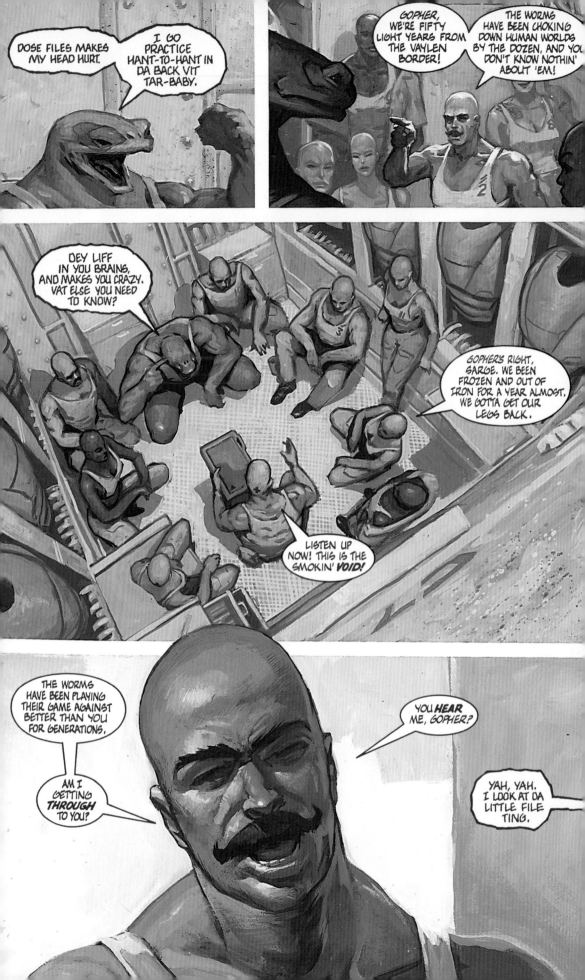

THE *MUNDUS HUMANITAS* TEMPLE ON THE FORTRESS-WORLD *HOTOK*.

THE HIGH COUNCIL SHOULD HAVE LET US CHOOSE OUR OWN MAN. KESLING WAS SPLENDID AS INTERIM FOMAS!

KESLING'S DEAD VESLI.

BAH! IT'S AN *INSULT!* THEY TREAT US LIKE THEIR CATTLE!

IT'S A MOOT POINT ANYWAY. WE'RE IN NO POSITION TO BLOCK THIS NEW MAN'S APPOINTMENT.

I'M SURE HE'LL BE AS COOPERATIVE AS KESLING ONCE HE LEARNS HOW THE LAND LIES.

MORE LIKELY HE'LL BE A POWDERED, MINCING FOP. HIS PERFUME WILL GIVE US ALL HEADACHES--

DON'T BE RIDICULOUS. THE COUNCIL DOESN'T BANISH SOMEONE FOR BEING TOO COOPERATIVE--

-- OR TOO FASHIONABLE.

I'LL WAGER HE MADE AN ENEMY OF SOMEONE HE SHOULDN'T HAVE, AND HOTOK'S HIS PENALTY.

WHAT DO YOU MEAN?

I MEAN THAT THEY'RE GETTING RID OF THE MAN, GEITAN, SENDING HIM AS FAR AWAY AS POSSIBLE!

SO HE'S A TROUBLEMAKER, IT MEANS NOTHING.

THE COUNCIL IS LIGHT YEARS AWAY! WE ARE THE POWER HERE! *WE* ARE!

KSSSHT
I THOUGHT YOU WERE GOING TO GEAR DOWN ON THE BRIDGE, FOMAS.
IT REEKS OF HIGH BREEDING UP THERE. COMING OUT'S HARD ENOUGH ON THE STOMACH AS IT IS.
FINAL WARNING. ALL SECTIONS REPORT IN.
GREEN LIGHT IN THE HOLD.
YOU RATS READY?
ALL SECTIONS SECURE, CAPTAIN.
VERY GOOD. CLOSE THE DRIVE ON MY MARK...
HELL YES!
HELL YES.

THE SHIFT GRABS MY HEART
AND TWISTS IT-- TRIES TO
PUSH IT UP MY THROAT.

"IT'S *HIS* FEET THAT ARE TAKING
YOU AWAY FROM ME, TREVOR."

THE HARNESS GRINDS, ITS
ROLLERS KNEADING MY AB-
DOMEN LIKE BREAD. IT
HELPS SOME.

"IT'S *HIS* HANDS ON THE CHISEL,
CARVING OUT *HIS* FATE."

BLOOD SURGES THROUGH
MY SKULL, BEHIND MY
EYES. I START TO
BLACK OUT.

AND THEN I'M RISING ON A
WAVE OF FLICKERING HEAT--
UP-- UP THE BURNING WHEEL.

AMID THE ROAR OF FLAMES A
VOICE IS SCREAMING, HOWLING
LIKE AN ANIMAL.

I BLACK OUT--

COTAR-FOMAS FAITH?
THE STARPORT'S CALLED CAPITAL MAIN. IT'S BIGGER THAN I EXPECTED.
IT MUST BE WELL INTO HOTOK'S FALLING SEASON. THE WIND RIPPING ACROSS THE OPEN TARMAC IS WILD AND COLD. BREAKERS CRASH IN THE DISTANCE.
I'M GEIL CARCAJOU.
SHE'S PRETTY IN A SHARP KIND OF WAY. SHE'S GOT MERISSA'S EYES...
I'M ARCHCOTARE MIABOLO'S RAVILAR. PERHAPS YOU'VE READ MY CHRONICLE "CENTURY OF LUST"?

NO KIDDING.

WAKE UP, HOTOK!

I THINK I'VE GOT A PRIEST UP HERE WHO SPEAKS HIS MIND!

KLAK

YOU'RE A DYING BREED, YOU KNOW. TAKE YOUR PREDECESSOR KESLING, FOR EXAMPLE.

THUNK

A MAN OF DELICATE SENSIBILITIES, A LOVER OF BEAUTY, OF NATURE-- FANCIED HIMSELF SOMETHING OF A POET. DROVE ME *CRAZY!*

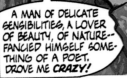

HE'D TALK OUT OF BOTH SIDES OF HIS MOUTH...

OUT THE BACK OF HIS HEAD EVEN, BEFORE HE'D TELL YOU SOMETHING STRAIGHT.

BUT *YOU* NOW, YEAH, OLD COGITO'S GOING TO *HATE* YOU.

KESLING?

HOW DID HE DIE?

IT WAS A NASTY END. ONE I WOULDN'T WISH ON ANYBODY.

ON THE OTHER HAND, IT MAKES FOR A GOOD STORY, AND A RAVILAR'S GOT TO EARN HER CRUST LIKE EVERYONE ELSE...

"THEY FOUND HIM ON THE ROCKS OFF HARVEST POINT."

"HE'D BEEN BATTERED SO BADLY HE WAS NEARLY UNRECOGNIZABLE. THEY SAID HE'D BEEN IN THE WATER MOST OF THE NIGHT."

GHKNFF HMFF

"THEY ALL TALKED ABOUT THE SMELL. A SWEETNESS, LIKE BRINE-ROTTEN FISH..."

IT MUST HAVE BEEN MEMORABLE, THOSE FISHERMEN ARE A PUNGENT LOT THEMSELVES!

HEE HEE!

"ANYWAY, WHEN THEY DRAGGED HIM ONTO THE BOAT, HE WAS CRAWLING WITH LITTLE WHITE CRABS."

"COMPLETELY COVERED. IF THEY HADN'T FOUND HIM BY THAT AFTERNOON, THERE WOULDN'T HAVE BEEN ANYTHING LEFT BUT HIS BOOTS."

CHUFF

WAS HE MURDERED?

NOBODY KNOWS. HE WAS LAST SEEN THE EVENING BEFORE HIS DEATH, CHECKING THROUGH SECURITY AT THE STARPORT.

DID HE HAVE ENEMIES?

KESLING? I DON'T THINK SO.

THE CHURCH OF THE TRANSITION MAYBE...

WHO?

NASTY, SQUALID LITTLE SECT. THEY WORSHIP STONES, OR SOME SUCH NONSENSE.

THE LOCALS EAT IT UP, OF COURSE. IDIOTS. BUT WHAT DO YOU EXPECT, WHEN THE LORD STEWARD HIMSELF IS A BELIEVER?

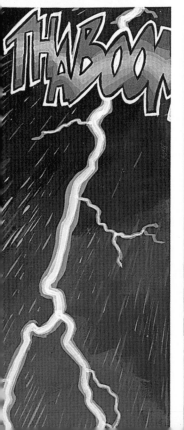

THE WIND CLAWS AT ME, FLAPPING ITS COLD WINGS AGAINST MY FACE.

SOMETHING INSIDE WRITHES LIKE A KNOT OF SNAKES.

AN ANOINTMENT.

SHHSHH SHHSHHSHH

MONKEY KING SCREECHES FROM MY LOINS, KICKING, STAMPING HIS HAIRY FEET.

"YOU HAVE LARGE EYES, DEMON, BUT YOU CANNOT SEE!

YOU THINK I'M SMALL, BUT I CAN DRAG THE MOON FROM HEAVEN WITH MY BARE HANDS!"

WHAT'S HE DOIN' NOW, SULLY?

HE JUST *THREW* SOMETHIN'.

SPAT

WHAT IS IT, SULLY?

I'LL BE JIGGERED! A TIN OF SMOKES!

BEAUTIFUL IRON, HALBART. WHAT GUILD IS IT?

AN EARTH GUILD. HOUSE OF TRIAM. THE BASIC CAST WAS LAID DOWN IN 340 BY THE MASTER HIMSELF.

MOST OF THE ARTIFICES ARE STILL ORIGINAL. IT'S A VERY RESPONSIVE, VERY SMOOTH JOB.

WHAT'S THIS PORT FOR?

THAT JACKS IN THE AVATAR. THE HEAVY DETECTION STUFF, YOU KNOW.

ANTITANK SYSTEMS: RADAR; LADAR; COUNTERBATTERY.

WHAT'S THIS MONKEY HERE?

THAT'S THE FOMAG' PERSONAL SIGNET.

REALLY?

WHAT'S THE SNAKE REPRESENT?

THAT'S THE RICHAERT CREST. THIS SUIT WAS PASSED DOWN TO THE FOMAS FROM HIS FATHER.

HE'S A NOBLE?

KRRK

THAT'S RIGHT. BARON RICHAERT WAS A REACHER LORD UP NORTH.

HE HELD TITLES ON FIVE WORLDS IN LUNIS SECTOR.

WHAT HAPPENED?

I MEAN, WHY IN LAHK'S NAME WOULD A BARON'S SON ENTER THE CHURCH?

WELL MA'AM, THAT'D BE THE FOMAS' BUSINESS, WOULDN'T IT?

COME NOW, HALBART. *YOU* MUST KNOW HIS MIND!

A STENTOR'S CONCERN IS WITH HIS PATRON'S IRON, MA'AM, NOT HIS MIND.

clink

SHSHSHSHSH

SSS

AH, WHAT A LOVELY BRIGHT MORNING IT IS.

WE'RE VERY GLAD TO HAVE YOU HERE TREVOR MY BOY, YES INDEED.

I'M SURE YOU'LL FIT RIGHT IN.

HOW FLATTERING THAT THE HIGH COUNCIL THOUGHT ENOUGH OF OUR LITTLE ENCLAVE TO SEND ONE OF THEIR OWN TO TAKE COMMAND OF THE GUARD.

YOUR PREDECESSOR, COTAR-FOMAS ROUTHY-- I LIKED HIM VERY MUCH. HE WAS MY TRUE FRIEND AND COMPANION.

WHEN HE PASSED ON, THE DREGUTAI THOUGHT I OUGHT TO PROMOTE YOUNG KESLING TO THE POST, PENDING YOUR ARRIVAL FROM THE THEOCRACY.

I SEE.

THEY GOT ON WELL WITH HIM, BUT I THOUGHT HE WAS A BIT OF A DISSEMBLER. DO YOU KNOW? A FLATTERER.

T5K

OF COURSE, THEY KNOW WHAT'S BEST. COULDN'T DO A THING AROUND HERE WITHOUT MY DREGUTAI!

AND KESLING'S SPARK HAS JOINED THE GREAT LIGHT. THERE'S NO EVIL LEFT IN HIM NOW.

"I BREAK WITH THEE AND WITH THY FATHER."

"PRAISE AHMILAHK."

EXCELLENCY, I UNDERSTAND THERE'S A HERETIC SECT ON HOTOK, PREACHING AGAINST THE TRUE FAITH.

I ASSUME THAT MEASURES ARE UNDER WAY TO SUPPRESS THEM...

NEVER MIND THAT, MY BOY. SAVE IT FOR LATER.

THESE GARDENS ARE *SO* LOVELY, EVEN IN THIS DISMAL FALLING SEASON.

IT REMINDS US OF OUR SACRED DUTY TREVOR... "TO TEND TO THE ETERNAL SOUL THAT IT MAY FLOURISH."

IS OUR FLESH A SUITABLE LANTERN FOR THE SECRET FIRE? SUCH WAS THE WISH OF THE PROPHET.

LEARN FROM THESE LOVELY WHITE *GENZERS* HERE. THEY ARE THE GREAT LIGHT MANIFEST IN THE PHYSICAL WORLD.

SKEEE

EXCELLENCY, IF YOU'LL EXCUSE ME, I'VE ARRANGED TO REVIEW THE GUARD IN A QUARTER HOUR ...

MY BOY, YOU'VE ONLY *JUST* ARRIVED!

YOU *REALLY* OUGHT TO SLOW YOUR TEMPO A BIT. TAKE TIME TO NURTURE YOUR SPIRIT. CULTIVATE A SENSE OF GRACE AND CALM. THE WHEEL TURNS AT ITS OWN PACE.

YOUR BIRDS TEACH A HARSH LESSON, EXCELLENCY.

OH! OH!

THE BLOCKHOUSE HAS BEEN CLEARED, AND THE GUARD IS LINED UP IN NEAT ROWS, LIKE TOY SOLDIERS.

I'VE BROUGHT THE GREY RATS WITH ME TO SHOW THEM WHAT REAL FIGHTERS LOOK LIKE.

THAT'S GOOD RIGHT THERE.

I THINK WE'RE READY NOW.

CAPTAIN SHOYAN, BY ORDER OF THE HIGH COUNCIL OF KUDUS, I ASSUME COMMAND OF THE HOTOK TEMPLE GUARD.

COTAR-FOMAS, THE GUARD IS YOURS AND READY FOR INSPECTION.

SHOW ME YOUR TOY SOLDIERS, YOU FAT BASTARD. SHOW ME YOUR PRETTY TOYS.

WE ARE AN ENTIRELY GRAV-MOBILE FORCE, FOMAS.

THIS IS FIRST COMPANY, IRON.

SECOND COMPANY, ARMORED INFANTRY.

THIRD COMPANY, CAVALRY, WITH BATTALION ASSETS.

THE TROOPS ARE GOOD MATERIAL -- GIVE THEM A FEW MONTHS AND THEY'LL SHAKE DOWN FINE.

YOU SEEM LIKE HEALTHY ENOUGH DOGS, BUT I WANT TO SEE YOU BITE!

THERE WILL BE LIVE-FIRE EXERCISES BY COMPANY BEGINNING AT 1200 HOURS TOMORROW. YOUR COMPANY COMMANDERS WILL BRIEF YOU ON THE TIMES AND PLACES.

DISMISSED.

SHOYAN AND HIS OFFICERS ON THE OTHER HAND...

THE WORST KIND OF FRONTIER GARBAGE. A BUNCH OF SELF-SATISFIED GRUBS WHO HAVEN'T BEEN IN IRON FOR YEARS.

MAY WE HAVE A MOMENT WITH YOU, COTAR?

SORRY. I'VE GOT BUSINESS IN TOWN TO ATTEND TO.

WE REPRESENT THE *DREGUTAI*, COTAR. YOUR BUSINESS CAN *WAIT*.

IS THAT RIGHT?

I REMEMBER YOU.

YOU WERE BOWING AND SCRAPING WITH THAT PACK OF BEATEN DOGS IN THE GARDEN THIS MORNING.

PLEASE PARDON MY COLLEAGUE'S ABRUPTNESS, COTAR-FOMAS.

WE'VE SIMPLY COME TO WELCOME YOU TO YOUR NEW HOME.

UNDER OUR HUMBLE GUIDANCE THIS TEMPLE HAS KNOWN HARMONY AND FELLOWSHIP. WE ARE A BLESSED FAMILY...

THE COTARS, HOLY CHILDREN, BOUND TOGETHER IN GLAD BROTHERHOOD...

...THE DREGUTAI, LOVING AND BENEVOLENT FATHERS.

DO YOU KNOW IT WAS THE DREGUTAI ON KUDAS THAT GOT ME SENT TO THIS HELL-HOLE IN THE FIRST PLACE.

"I FEEL THE SNAKES COILING AGAIN, CRUSHING MY LUNGS."

KESLING WAS YOUR GILDED BIRD, WASN'T HE? YOU WOUND HIM UP AND HE SANG PRETTY SONGS FOR YOU.

WELL, I TAKE MY ORDERS FROM THE ARCHCOTARE. *PERIOD.*

YOU KEEP CLEAR OF MY BUSINESS, AND I'LL KEEP CLEAR OF YOURS.

I'M AFRAID IT'S NOT THAT *SIMPLE*, MY BOY.

FOLLOW THE ARCHCOTARE'S ADVICE. LEARN TO BE HUMBLE.

"A MAN WITH A SENSIBLE NATURE FINDS THAT FATE ROLLS WITH HIM."

IS THAT SO.

ABSOLUTELY.

"THE ONLY SLAVE IS A WILLING ONE."

THERE'S ANOTHER PROVERB FOR YOU.

THAT'S RIGHT.

I THOUGHT THEY'D BE QUARTERING YOU AT THE TEMPLE...

I'M OFF-WORLD A LOT. IT'S MORE CONVENIANT TO RENT A CELL NEAR THE MAIN.

CAN I GET YOU SOMETHING? YOU LOOK KINDA SICK.

NO. I'M FINE.

COURTNEY WAS A GOOD MAN. HOW'S HE DOING?

ALRIGHT. HE'S GOT A DIRTSIDE JOB ON DAKLEAH WITH THE FLEET.

HIS HEART STARTED SEIZING UP DURING THE HEx SHIFTS. SPENT A COUPLE OF YEARS IN TREATMENT FOR IT ACTUALLY.

HE TOLD ME YOU WERE A HOT PILOT IN THE OLD DAYS.

THANKS.

YEAH... THE OLD DAYS.

I STILL DO SOME SCOUTING WORK FOR BARON BERNEDOTH--THE LORD STEWARD.

I BOUGHT MY OWN SHIP AFTER "LUST" CAME OUT.

THE SILVER ORCHID. I GOT HER NEW OUT OF THE BENEA SHIPYARDS.

YOU INTERESTED IN AN EARLY DINNER?

I KNOW A GOOD GRESCI HOUSE, RIGHT ON THE HARBOR.

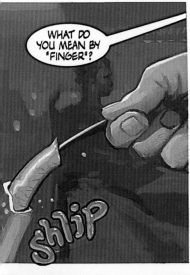

WHAT DO YOU MEAN BY "FINGER"?

SHLIP

IT'S JUST JARGON. THE VAYLEN WILL PACK A COMMERCIAL MERC-ATOR WITH SENSORS AND SEND IT SCOUTING INTO THE EMPIRE.

FINGERS GATHER INFORMATION, FEEL OUT OUR DEFENSES.

AND THERE ARE MORE OF THEM AROUND THESE DAYS?

MMM... YEAH.

I HIT ONE MYSELF A COUPLE OF MONTHS AGO, NOSING AROUND NEAR PHIEBUS.

THE BASTARDS HIT ME WITH NAILS AND SCAMPERED. NEARLY TORE THE ORCHID IN HALF!

I HEARD YESTERDAY THAT LORD MORIKEAN CAUGHT 'EM. THE WHOLE CREW'D BEEN HULLED.

THEY WERE VAYLEN?

THEY WERE HUMAN BEINGS TREVOR. PEOPLE LIKE YOU AND ME.

THERE WERE WORMS INSIDE THEM, YEAH, BUT THEY WERE PEOPLE.

THE WORMS ARE GOING TO GET US ALL SOONER OR LATER.

WHAT CAN YOU TELL ME ABOUT THESE VAYLEN?

I KNOW THAT THEY CONTROL NERVE IMPULSES; THAT THEY USE OUR BRAINS TO KICK-START THEIR OWN SENTIENCE...

THEY'RE UGLY LITTLE THINGS. KIND OF LIKE WHAT WE'RE EATING.

TREVOR, THERE ARE VERY FEW OF US WHO HAVEN'T LOST SOMEONE THEY LOVE TO THE WORMS...

WE DON'T TALK ABOUT THEM MUCH. NOT POLITE CONVERSATION.

COTAR • FOMAS

CHAPTER 2: INQUISITION

IT'S NOT SO DIFFERENT HERE. WHAT YOU'VE HEARD IS TRUE. OF COURSE THE METROPOLITAN'S COURT GLITTERS WITH GOLD... MOSUM SHINES IN SPACE LIKE A SPHERE OF DIAMONDS...

BUT THE THEOCRACY IS *ROTTEN*, GEIL. IT'S DYING INSIDE.

THE METROPOLITAN IS ISOLATED AND CORRUPT.

IF HE CARED TO LOOK ABOUT HIM... TO CONSIDER WHAT'S HAPPENING TO THE ORDINARY PEOPLE UPON WHOSE BACKS THE GLORY OF MOSUM WAS BUILT...

BUT HE DOESN'T CARE TO LOOK. THE COURT PLAYS ITS PETTY GAMES AND THE WORLDS *BLEED*, TORN APART BY DOGS DRAWN TO THE SCENT OF DEATH.

GOODNESS!

LOOK AROUND YOU, GEIL. IT'S THE SAME *EVERYWHERE* IN THE REALM.

EMPIRE... THEOCRACY... THERE'S NO DIFFERENCE.

YET YOU LEFT THE EMPIRE TO JOIN THE CHURCH...

DID YOU KNOW THAT I'M A BARON'S SON?

WELL... YES, ACTUALLY. YOUR STENTOR LET IT SLIP.

MY FATHER FOUGHT LIKE AN ANIMAL TO "RISE" OUT OF THE COMMON CROWD HE'D HAVE DONE ANYTHING... *ANYTHING* TO HAVE BEEN ACCEPTED BY THE LOCAL BLOOD.

HE FOUGHT FANATICALLY DURING THE CRUSADES.

AFTER THE SIEGE OF BALDON, DUKE NAIFA WAS FORCED TO ACKNOWLEDGE HIM.

HE THREW US A FEW SCRAPS OF LAND ON SOME RAPED AND FROZEN PLANETS.

FATHER GNAWED THAT BONE AS IF IT WERE A *BANQUET*, DENYING THE HUMILIATION OF IT.

"SON," HE'D SAY, "YOU'RE PART OF A MIGHTY HOUSE NOW. ALWAYS UPHOLD YOUR FAMILY'S HONOR!"

BLINDNESS! TO THE GENTRY IT WAS ALL A SICK JOKE. FATHER WAS ENTIRELY IN THEIR POWER. HE'D DANCE FOR THEM, LICK THEIR SPIT OFF THE FLOOR--

--AS LONG AS HE COULD BE ONE OF THEM.

POOR MAN...

HE WAS A DELUDED *FOOL.* THAT'S ALL.

WHEN HE DIED, COURTNEY INHERITED THE TITLE, AND I LEFT. I ABANDONED MY...

...WELL, I *LEFT.* I SHIPPED INTO THE THEOCRACY AND AFTER A COUPLE OF YEARS WANDERING, I CAME TO THE CHURCH.

I DON'T KNOW. I WAS TIRED. MAYBE I WANTED TO BE *PART* OF SOMETHING AGAIN.

LIGHTWAY. IT'S ALWAYS PACKED AT WEEK'S END.

OH! I'VE BEEN WANTING TO TRY THAT ONE ON.

HOW DO YOU THINK I'D LOOK AS A BLONDE?

WHAT... YOU'RE *CORVUS?*

SO I DON'T SHOW IT OFF LIKE YOU DO. I'VE HAD MY CRUCIS SINCE '87.

"FERRARIA DOMINA," THE IRON LADY. YOU GOT THIS IN THE FLEET.

HOW ABOUT THAT.

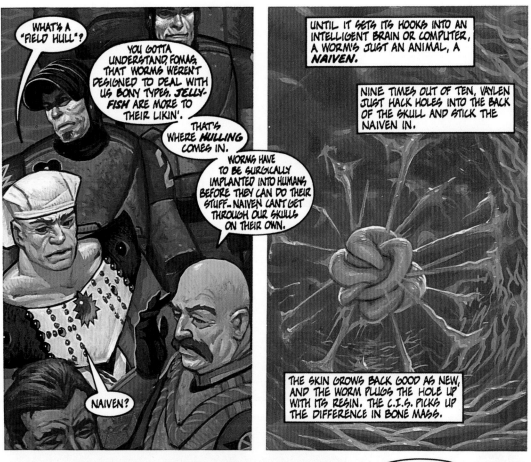

WHAT'S A "FIELD HULL"?

YOU GOTTA UNDERSTAND, FONAS, THAT WORMS WEREN'T DESIGNED TO DEAL WITH US BONY TYPES. *JELLY-FISH* ARE MORE TO THEIR LIKIN'.

THAT'S WHERE *HULLING* COMES IN.

WORMS HAVE TO BE SURGICALLY IMPLANTED INTO HUMANS BEFORE THEY CAN DO THEIR STUFF... NAIVEN CAN'T GET THROUGH OUR SKULLS ON THEIR OWN.

NAIVEN?

UNTIL IT SETS ITS HOOKS INTO AN INTELLIGENT BRAIN OR COMPUTER, A WORM'S JUST AN ANIMAL, A *NAIVEN.*

NINE TIMES OUT OF TEN, VAYLEN JUST HACK HOLES INTO THE BACK OF THE SKULL AND STICK THE NAIVEN IN.

THE SKIN GROWS BACK GOOD AS NEW, AND THE WORM PLUGS THE HOLE UP WITH ITS RESIN. THE C.I.S. PICKS UP THE DIFFERENCE IN BONE MASS.

LAHK'S BLOOD...

DAMN *RIGHT.* A SLICK HULLIN' JOB'S HARDER TO PICK UP. THEY SLIP YOUNG WORMS IN ALONG THE OPTIC NERVE, LET 'EM GROW IN THE BRAIN FLUID.

OR THEY USE SPECIAL DEVICES TO FEED ADULTS IN ALONGSIDE THE SPINAL CORD.

THOSE ARE TOUGHER TO PICK UP BECAUSE THERE'S NO SKULL BREACH. BUT YOU *DON'T* SEE MANY OF THOSE, SIR, THOSE ARE THE *FANCY JOBS.*

ᔓᔓᔓᔓᔓᔓ

IS THAT THE LORD STEWARD?

RIGHT YOU ARE, SIR. LORD GEVAS DO BERNEDOTH.

THE SNAKE FIVE STEPS BELOW HIM IS TARRAK FIKE, COMMANDER OF THE CHOT GUARD.

OH YES? TELL ME ABOUT HIM.

LITTLE TO SAY, SIR, AND *NONE* OF IT GOOD. HE'S SLIPPERY AS AN ALE-WIFE.

WHAT DOES HIS COMMAND RATE?

CLAP CLAP

AN ANVIL BATTALION. HIS HAMMER'S NOTHIN' MORE THAN A COUPLE OF BEAT UP OLD MERCATORS AND TUGS.

TECH INDEX IS AROUND 4. PRETTY UNEVEN. HIS IRON COMPANY'S SUPPOSED TO BE GOOD.

THE LINE COMPANIES ARE *DIRT* FROM WHAT I HEAR.

CHURCH OF THE TRANSITION
GRAV-INFANTRY BATTALION (FORGED)

IRON   LINE

CLAP
CLAP
CLAP

THERE'S THE CONSTABLE.

COME ON!

OH!

CRETIN!

ON THE DOUBLE, LADS!

THE SHIPMENT WILL BE COMING IN THROUGH CAPITAL MAIN, WE COULDN'T GET CLEARANCE FOR THE TEMPLE PAD.

VERY WELL, I'LL TAKE THE GARNE'S PLATOON AND ESCORT IT IN MYSELF.

LET'S PRAY THERE AREN'T ANY MORE INCONVENIENCES.

NO SIR.

IT LOOKS LIKE THE MUNDAS HAS FOUND ITSELF A NEW COTAR-FOMAS, SIR.

MMM... YES. A SORRY CHOICE IF HIS PERFORMANCE TODAY IS ANY INDICATION. MUSCLING HIS WAY THROUGH THE CROWD LIKE AN ERRANT BULL...

ACH! I LEFT MY GLOVES IN THE CHANCEL... I WON'T BE A MOMENT...

COMMANDER FIKE.

YEAH, YOUR GLOVES.

AN EAVESDROPPER AS WELL AS A BOOR... ONE BEGINS TO SUSPECT THAT OLD MIABOLO'S HIRED A STREET TOUGH.

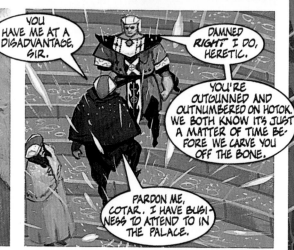

YOU HAVE ME AT A DISADVANTAGE, SIR.

DAMNED *RIGHT* I DO, HERETIC. YOU'RE OUTGUNNED AND OUTNUMBERED ON HOTOK. WE BOTH KNOW IT'S JUST A MATTER OF TIME BEFORE WE CARVE YOU OFF THE BONE.

PARDON ME, COTAR. I HAVE BUSINESS TO ATTEND TO IN THE PALACE.

MAYBE, YOU'RE RIGHT.

AND MAYBE "OLD MIABOLO" MADE THE SMARTEST MOVE OF OF HIS LIFE BRINGING ME HERE.

STILL, IT'S A RARE PRIEST THESE DAYS WHO DOESN'T KEEP A BOUGHT GIRL OR TWO IN THE CLOSET--

TONIGHT I'M LOOKING FOR SOMEONE WHO'S CLOSE TO FIKE ...

...*REAL* CLOSE.

MMMF!

HOO! THAT PRIEST'S DISC MUST BE FILLED TO THE GILLS, KRUTE. MEBBE WE'D OUGHTA *LIGHTEN* HIS LOAD A BIT!!

BEAT IT, ANNA!

WELL NOW, FELLA.

I WAS JUST TELLIN' *KRUTE* HERE THAT YOU SEEMED LIKE A MAN IN NEED OF SOME ASSISTANCE.

KIERUTANA LIKE BOY'S NECKLACE...

A MUKHADISH. A *TROLL.* BRED BY THE VAYLEN AS WORKHORSES AFTER THE KERRN DISASTER. THEY PROVED MORE DOCILE...

KIERUTANA TINK BOY SHOULD GIVE KIERUTANA PRETTY NECKLACE...

BUT THAT'S STILL JUST A MATTER OF DEGREES. IF GOPHER AND THIS MONSTER EVER SAW EACH OTHER THEY'D LEVEL HALF A BLOCK BE- TWEEN THEM.

clink

KERRNS AND TROLLS ARE LIKE SODIUM AND WATER... OTHER- WISE INERT MATTER THAT EX- PLODES ON CONTACT...

S ONE SEEMS MORE RT THAN USUAL. CKY FOR ME--

KRUTE, LOOK OUT!

SUNRISE OVER THE NORTH HILLS TESTING RANGE.

KRUMP

THE DISCHARGE OF THE IFV'S *FUSION GUN* FEELS LIKE IT'S TEARING FLESH FROM MY SCALP.

THE SHARP **CRACK** OF THE BOLT IS FOLLOWED INSTANTS LATER BY A ROLLING ROAR AS COOL AIR RUSHES IN ALONG THE BOLT'S TRACK.

WHOOM

ENERGIZED PLASMA, CRASH-ING INTO THE FAR RIDGE, *BLASTS* THE FROZEN SOIL SKYWARD IN A BLACK SPOUT OF MUD AND STEAM...

SECOND PLATOON HAULS IN LOW OVER THE NEAR SLOPE AS THE COVERING FIRE SLACKENS.

R RRII PPPP

MOVE IT! *MOVE IT!*

FIRST PLATOON AIR-DROPS *DIRECTLY* OVER THE TAR-GET, DANGEROUS IN THIS TERRAIN.

TROOPS IN IRON PELT IN-TO THE TREELINE LIKE ARMORED *HAILSTONES*...

SMASH

CRASH

10

BASH

YOU THE PRIEST? I DIDN'T KNOW THEY **CAME** IN YOUR SIZE!

I'M TREVOR FAITH. WHO ARE YOU?

LUPIS. YOU CAN CALL ME **LOOP.**

OFFICIALLY I'M CARCAJOUS GUNNER, BUT YOU KNOW HOW IT IS... I'M ALSO HER STENTOR, ENGINEER, LOVE-SLAVE...

Spat

LOOP, YOU WERE SUPPOSED TO BE **GONE** BY NOW.

WOLFIE, I'VE BEEN GONE FOR **YEARS.**

SSSSSS

WHAT'S THAT SUPPOSED TO MEAN?

AS LONG AS LOOP'S BEEN WITH ME, I **STILL** DON'T UNDERSTAND HALF OF WHAT HE SAYS.

BUT HE'S A GOOD HAND AND THAT MAKES UP FOR A LOT.

YOU SAID YOU HAD SOMETHING I'D FIND INTERESTING...

MAYBE, MAYBE **NOT.**

KESLING'S *DIARY*.

WHAT!? HOW DID *YOU* GET THIS?

LIKE I TOLD YOU BEFORE, KESLING THOUGHT HE WAS A GREAT POET.

WE USED TO LINK COMPUTERS. HE'D DOWNLOAD HIS TRASH FOR ME TO READ-- *AWFUL* STUFF.

BUT THE REST OF HIS FILE WAS THERE TOO, NIGHT AFTER NIGHT, BEGGING ME TO FLIP THROUGH IT.

I SUCCUMBED TO TEMPTATION, NOTICED A FOLDER LABELED *"JOURNAL"* AND COPIED IT.

GEIL, WHY ARE YOU TELLING ME THIS? IF THE *DREGUTAI* FIND OUT YOU'VE STOLEN THIS, YOU COULD BE BANNED FROM THE TEMPLE.

I CAN'T ACCESS THE FOLDER ON MY COMPUTER. IT'S GOT SOME KIND OF LOCK-OUT.

YOU'RE THE NEW FOMAS. MAYBE IT'LL OPEN FOR YOU.

LOOK, I'M CURIOUS. CAN YOU BLAME ME? I WANT TO KNOW IF KESLING WAS *MURDERED!*

HOTOK FORTRESS AT SUNRISE.

..."THE KEEP."

ITS CHAMBERS AND BUNKERS STRETCH FOR KILOMETERS IN ALL DIRECTIONS, STITCHED TO THE MAIN POWER SINK BY CABLES AND GRID CHANNELS.

N5

CLOUDS OF SMOKE HEAVE FROM ITS SPIRES LIKE BLACK PENNONS IN THE WIND --

-- AND AT ITS CENTER, Q-BEAMS SQUAT IN THEIR ARMORED SILOS, READY TO SCOURGE THE HEAVENS.

EIL'S RIGHT. HOTOK FORTRESS S KILLING THIS WORLD; DRINK-JG ITS LIFE-BLOOD; SPEWING LTH ON ITS FACE.

HOTOK IS A *SACRIFICE*...

OUR TALISMAN AGAINST DEMONS THAT HUNGER IN THE DARK...

..."YOU'LL ASSEMBLE YOUR FORCES AT THE STAGING AREA ON DAY 131. THAT GIVES YOU THREE MONTHS OF PREPARATION.

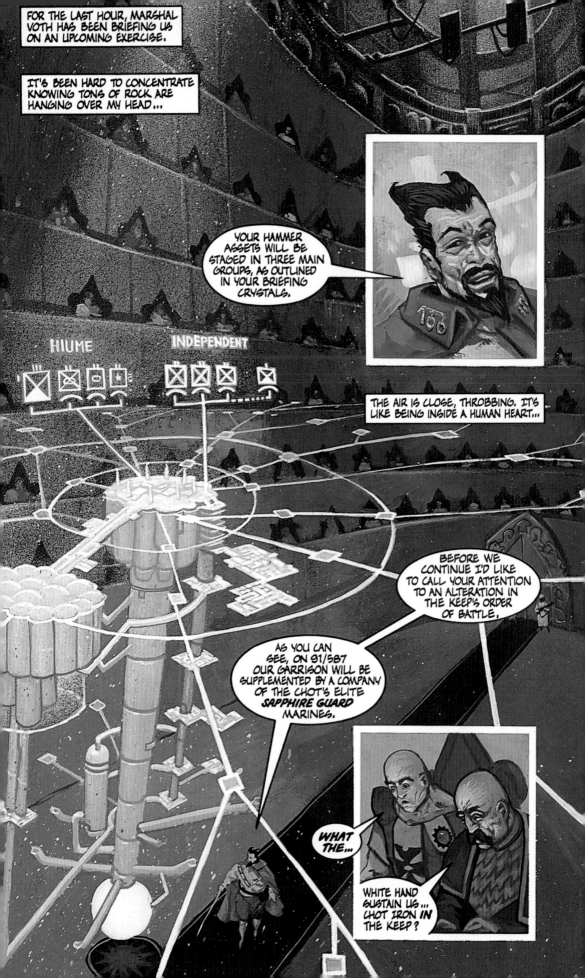

WHAT!?

HAS BERNEDOTH SUDDEN-LY GONE *MAD!?* THE CHOT ARE DEMON-SPAWN... *HERET-ICS!* TO PLACE THEM IN SUCH A VITAL SPOT--

--INDEED, IN THE VERY *HEART* OF OUR DEFENSES! IT IS THE *WILDEST FOLLY!*

EXCELLENCY, CALM YOURSELF...

CALM!

I'LL KNOW NOT CALM, NOR *PEACE* WHILE THIS *IDIOT RULES!* IT'S TIME HE WAS BROUGHT TO HEEL...

EXCELLENCY!

HE'S RIGHT, DREGUS. THE CHOT HAVE *POISONED* THE LORD STEWARD'S COUNSEL.

WE MUST *DESTROY THEM* BEFORE THEY CORRUPT OTHERS.

THE CHOT HAVE GONE UN-OPPOSED FOR TOO LONG ON HOTOK.

IT'S *PAST TIME* WE MOVED AGAINST THEM...

ENOUGH, COTAR!

THIS SITUATION CALLS FOR CAREFUL CONSIDERATION, NOT BLIND FURY!

EXCELLENCY, I PROPOSE WE RECESS UNTIL TOMORROW, WHEN PASSIONS HAVE COOLED.

I ... I MUST MEDITATE.

WE WILL RECONVENE IN THE MORNING WHEN I HAVE CONSIDERED THE MATTER FULLY.

I CAN ALMOST HEAR THE OLD MAN'S CHAINS CLANK-ING AS HE LEAVES.

THERE'S AN OILY GLISTEN OF POISON IN COGITO'S EYES. HE'S JUST *WAITING* FOR HIS CHANCE TO PUT THE KNIFE IN.

WHEN I LOAD IT INTO MY TERMINAL, KESLING'S FOLDER OPENS WITHOUT A HITCH.

ALL OF KESLING'S PERSONAL FILES HAD BEEN *EMPTIED* BEFORE MY ARRIVAL. POSSIBLY ROUTINE, POSSIBLY BECAUSE SOMEBODY DIDN'T WANT ME TO SEE THEM.

BLESS YOU AND YOUR INQUISITIVENESS, GEIL...

I SKIP OVER THE FIRST ENTRIES, UNTIL I BEGIN GETTING REFERENCES TO A *"SHIREA VENAN."*

SHE CAPTAINS THE MERCATOR *GISELLE* OUT OF TIMOK PRIME.

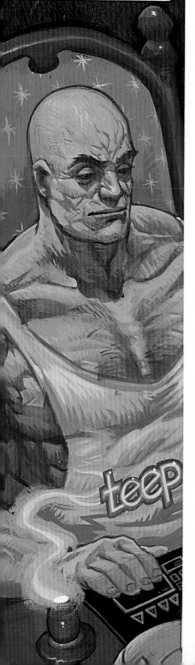

teep

teep
teep
teep

Day 338

Today, Shirea told me she *loved* me! The woman who's always been so careful not to give me the wrong idea tells me she *loves* me...

Day 341

Shirea's still holding back for some reason, although I know her feelings are genuine... is it the same kind of love I feel, or is it platonic... I don't know...

teep
teep

Day 346

Darkness is eating my heart... my soul is a wasteland of smoke and ash...

FIKE! She's left me for my worst enemy! *Bitch!* Scuttling vermin!

How could she have told me the things she did, and then gone to him?

Day 347

She's still bunking on the *Giselle*, but won't answer my messages.

She *must* tell me why she's done this. I deserve *that* much at least!

THE *LAST* ENTRY.

LAHK'S BLOOD...
SHE LEFT KESLING FOR TARRAK FIKE!

MIDNIGHT.

THE MUNDAS HUMANITAS HAS A PRIVATE HANGAR BAY AT CAPITAL MAIN.

INSIDE THE BAY'S PERIMETER, HULKING FORMS CROWD TOGETHER, BLOTTING OUT THE STARS.

ANVIL INSERTION CRAFT WITH STUBBY WINGS, HARDPOINTS HANGING FROM THEIR BELLIES LIKE STALACTITES.

HUGE MERCATORS SQUATTING LIKE BEETLES ON THEIR HYDRAULIC LEGS.

THE BAY IS QUIET AND DARK. THE WATCH OFFICER GIVES ME ACCESS TO HIS TERMINAL.

I DISCOVER THAT THE GISELLE IS STILL ON THE GROUND--

--THAT SHE WAS MOVED TO THE CHURCH OF THE TRANSITION'S PRIVATE BAY THE MORNING AFTER KESLING DIED--

--THAT THE ORDER WAS SUBMITTED BY SHIP'S LAPTAIN VENAN AND CO-SIGNED BY COMMANDER FIKE.

I PULL ON A "HEAT" JUMPSUIT, DESIGNED TO MIMIC MY THERMAL ENVIRONMENT.

IT WILL RENDER ME ALL BUT INVISIBLE TO PASSIVE IR SENSORS.

"WAITING NO LONGER, THE MONKEY-KING SHOOK HIMSELF AND VANISHED WITHOUT A TRACE."

"EHR-LANG SEARCHED FOR HIM HIGH AND LOW, BUT THE MONKEY-KING HAD SLIPPED AWAY, INTO THE DEMON'S TEMPLE..."

I'M COMING, DEMON.

THE GISELLE IS PARKED IN AN OUT-OF-THE-WAY CORNER OF THE HANGAR, BEHIND A MOUNTAIN OF CRATES AND BOXES.

SHE'S AN ORDINARY-LOOKING MERCATOR. LOCKED DOWN TIGHT. NO SIGNS OF LIFE.

THE LOCK IS TECH INDEX 5 OR 6. GOREY'D MAKE SHORT WORK OF IT. HAVE TO BRING HER BACK HERE WITH ME.

A CHOT SLED. LET'S SEE WHO'S VISITING OUR MYSTERY LADY TONIGHT.

NO... *PLEASE*...

LAHK! THAT'S *TONSON*...

HE LOOKS LIKE HE'S BEEN *DRUGGED*.

AND THE ONE IN FRONT...

COTAR • FOMAS

CHAPTER 3: TREASON

SSSSHUSHHSSHH

TONSON--THE CHURCH OF THE TRANSITION'S ESTATE STEWARD.

LAST NIGHT, I WATCHED HIS SUPERIOR CARRY HIM, BOUND LIKE AN ANIMAL, INTO THE *GISELLE*.

THAT'S NOT SOMETHING ONE EXPECTS TO SEE--

HI THERE, RIVERMAN.

TONSON BROKE OUR DATE LAST NIGHT.

GROWWL... YOU'RE SOMETHING ELSE, YOU KNOW THAT?

MY OFFER STILL STANDS, RIVERMAN. YOU'LL NEVER PAY A COIN FOR THIS GIRL.

I STOOD FOR AN HOUR IN THOSE DAMNED BUSHES WAITING FOR TONSON TO SHOW.

I THINK HE WAS SCARED WE'D BE SEEN TOGETHER...

THE TEMPLE'S BEEN CRAWLING WITH PILGRIMS SINCE THE BIG RETREAT WAS CALLED.

IT DOESN'T START FOR ANOTHER WEEK YET, BUT THERE ARE ALREADY HUNDREDS OF PEOPLE CAMPED OUTSIDE THE GATE.

TRY AGAIN TONIGHT.

SURE. BUT HE WON'T SHOW. THE CROWD'S GOT HIM SPOOKED.

MY BROTHERS WERE ANIMALS... I WAS LUCKY TO HAVE ESCAPED CHILDHOOD AT ALL.

TREI WAS THE WORST. ONCE HE STARTED IN ON ME, HE WOULDN'T LET UP UNTIL HE SAW BLOOD.

FATHER WAS NEVER AROUND TO STOP HIM, AND I THINK MY MOTHER WAS AFRAID...

WHEN I WAS FIFTEEN, TREI KNOCKED MY LEFT EYE OUT. CLEAN OUT. THEY WERE ABLE TO SAVE IT--

--BUT I SWORE I'D KILL HIM FOR THAT.

DID YOU?

THE WORMS TOOK HIM FIRST.

WHAT'S THAT?

WHITE SOUND.

IF WE KEEP OUR VOICES DOWN, IT WILL MASK THEM. MICROPHONES TOO, UNLESS THEY'RE CONDUCTION IMPLANTS.

HMMMMMMMMMM

I COULD USE ONE OF THOSE AT NIGHT. LOOP SNORES LIKE A BULL ELEPHANT.

SO WHAT'S THE BIG SECRET?

I READ KESLING'S DIARY. I THINK HE WAS MURDERED.

I KNEW IT! I KNEW IT!

I'M GOING TO GET PROOF TONIGHT. I NEED SOMEONE WHO KNOWS HAMMERS TO COME WITH ME.

SOMEONE I CAN TRUST.

THAT'S THE *GISELLE*.

FIKE WENT IN THROUGH THE REAR VALVE LAST NIGHT, WE'LL TRY THAT FIRST.

NOTHIN' TO IT, FOMAS. GIMME FIVE MINUTES.

THE SHIP'S AN SM-70. PROBABLY LAID DOWN IN THE SEVENTIES. PRIVATE OPERATORS BUY THEM USED WHEN THE TRANSIT GUILDS UPGRADE.

SHE'S HAD HER DRIVE SKIRT BROADENED.

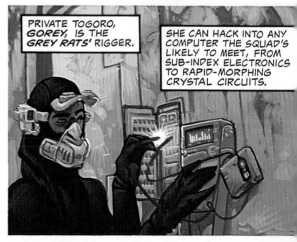

PRIVATE TOGORO, *GOREY*, IS THE *GREY RATS'* RIGGER.

SHE CAN HACK INTO ANY COMPUTER THE SQUAD'S LIKELY TO MEET, FROM SUB-INDEX ELECTRONICS TO RAPID-MORPHING CRYSTAL CIRCUITS.

THE VALVE HAD PARALLEL INDEX 6 COMPUTER LOCKS, FOMAS. I'VE OFF-LINED BOTH OF THEM.

GOOD WORK, *GOREY*. WE'RE COMING IN.

THE *GISELLE'S* ON MINIMUM POWER. JUST ENOUGH TO KEEP HER SYSTEMS ACTIVE.

EEP EEP

FSSSSSSS

GEIL?

THIS SHIP'S A VAYLEN *FINGER*. AND NOT JUST ANY FINGER EITHER. SHE'S OUTFITTED FOR SLAVING.

THIS IS A SURGERY... WHERE THEY *HULL* PEOPLE.

GOREY, I WANT VISUALS ON ALL OF THIS.

CHECK.

TEEP TEEP

THERE'S BLOOD OVER HERE. IT LOOKS PRETTY FRESH. A DAY OR TWO ON THE OUTSIDE.

IS THAT WHAT WAS GOING ON LAST NIGHT? FIKE BROUGHT TONSON IN HERE TO BE HULLED?

FOMAS, I'VE GOT SOMETHING--

--A POWERED CHAMBER UNDER THE DECK PLATES.

WHERE?

STOREROOM DOWN THE MAIN CORRIDOR.

FSSSHT

ZZZZTT

GIVE ME A SECOND.

VENTRAL DDU STORE

KLANG

THESE ARE HOST BODIES. KEPT ALIVE ON LIFE-SUPPORT--

--LIKE A VAYLEN WARDROBE.

THAT WOMAN IN THE CENTER IS SHEREA VENAN.

BUT IF THE WORM'S NOT INSIDE HER...

...WHERE IS IT?

IT'S ONLY WHEN WE'RE RUNNING BACK TO THE HANGAR THAT THE PATTERN EMERGES, SPREADING ITSELF BEFORE MY EAGER EYES...

THE MONKEY-KING SHRIEKS IN MY GUT... A WILD, CACKLING HOWL OF DELIGHT.

"...THE GARRISON WILL BE SUPPLEMENTED BY A COMPANY OF THE CHOT'S ELITE SAPPHIRE GUARD MARINES..."

"...I THINK IT HAS SOMETHING TO DO WITH THE TEMPLE HOSPITAL. MACHINES OR SOMETHING..."

GEIL, YOU SAID YOU HAVE A CONTRACT WITH THE LORD STEWARD... AS A SCOUT.

YEAH.

DO YOU CARRY A LETTER OF MARQUE?

A LIMITED ONE. BORDER LORDS CAN'T AFFORD TO FIGHT EACH OTHER WITH THE WORMS BREATHING DOWN THEIR NECKS.

LITERALLY.

BUT THE ORCHID IS ARMED AND YOU HAVE THE AUTHORITY TO GO AFTER VAYLEN SHIPS, RIGHT?

YEEESSS--

I CAN'T BOMBARD THE GISELLE FROM ORBIT, IF THAT'S WHAT YOU'RE GETTING AT. IT'S SITTING ON SOVEREIGN TERRITORY...

NO. BUT IN SPACE YOU CAN BOARD AND SEARCH SUSPECTED FINGERS.

ANY CHANCE I GET.

SSSSSSSSSSSSHHHH

AN ARCTIC WIND IS KEEPING EVERYONE INDOORS THIS MORNING. IT'S JUST DANNI AND I.

ALONE WITH THE RAGING RIVER.

I TAKE IT YOU MET TONSON LAST NIGHT. HOW DID HE SEEM?

HE WAS SORTA PREOCCUPIED. LIKE HE WASN'T REALLY IN THE ROOM WITH ME.

I ENDED UP GIVING HIM ONE OF MY FAMOUS MASSAGES WHILE HE SPILLED HIS GUTS.

AND THAT'S WHY I THOUGHT I SHOULD TALK TO YOU RIGHT AWAY...

HE TOLD ME THE SHIPMENT HAS FALLEN THROUGH, THE ONE HE'S BEEN WORKING SO LONG TO SET UP, AND HE'S TERRIFIED THAT IT'LL COST HIM HIS BENEFICE.

HE KEPT ON ABOUT IT ALL NIGHT, MOANING "IT'S BEEN CANCELED, IT'S BEEN CANCELED."

DANNI'S SITTING AT THE FAR END OF THE BENCH, HER HANDS IN HER LAP...

I THOUGHT YOU'D WANT TO KNOW.

SHE HASN'T TOUCHED ME ONCE...

SHE DOESN'T RESPOND IMMEDIATELY... MAYBE SHE'S JUST SURPRISED.

BUT I'D SWEAR IT'S SOMETHING MORE--

--SOMETHING DEEPER.

DANNI, I WANT YOU TO COME WITH ME.

I WANT TO STICK YOU UNDER ONE OF THOSE SKULL IMAGERS.

WHEN THE GUN SLAPS INTO HER HAND, I'M READY FOR IT...

SCHAK

I SHOVE HER OFF BALANCE, GIVING ME THE SECONDS I NEED TO FREE MY KUSARI.

BLAM

THE KNIFE BUCKS AS IT SPLITS THROUGH A PAIR OF RIBS. HER VOICE CHUCKLES WITH BLOOD.

CHOK

I WAIT FOR HER TO FALL.

SNICK

THKK

UHRK...

SHE DOESN'T.

CHH... CHH...

AAAH!

CHOK

SHE'S IN TOO CLOSE. I CAN'T SWING THE CHAIN...

I FEEL SOMETHING TEAR INTO ME AGAIN, SLIGHTLY HIGHER...

BUT THE BLADE STRIKES BONE, AND SHE'S NOT STRONG ENOUGH TO BREAK THROUGH...

THKK

I CAN FEEL THE WAIST OF MY JACKET FILLING WITH BLOOD...

MY ARMS ARE SHAKING. I HAVE TO LOCK THEM TO KEEP FROM PITCHING ON MY FACE.

DANNI'S WOUND SMACKS ITS RED LIPS, DROOLS BLOOD ONTO THE STONE PATH...

WHEN MY BLADE PIERCED HER HEART, EVEN THE MONSTER INSIDE HER COULDN'T IGNORE IT...

THE MONSTER...

I DON'T KNOW WHAT I EXPECT TO SEE--

--BUT IT ISN'T A BLOODY HOLE.

YIPE

YIPE

YOU LITTLE BASTARD.

YIPE

YIPE

IDIOT... CAUGHT IN MY OWN BLAST LIKE A RANK AMATEUR.

I HAVE JUST ENOUGH STRENGTH TO SIGNAL THE *RATS* BEFORE THE DARK SWEEPS ME AWAY...

FOMAS?

FOMAS!

TAR-BABY, WHAT'RE HIS COORDINATES?

FOMAS, YOU REST EASY, WE'RE ON OUR WAY.

I COME TO IN THE BLOCKHOUSE INFIRMARY. *DOC'S* STEADY FINGERS ARE PROBING MY SIDE.

THE FAMILIAR PRICKLING OF NANOSURGIC FOAM MEANS THAT I'M NOT IN SERIOUS TROUBLE.

SURFACE BURNS, BLOOD LOSS, AND A COUPLE OF CLEAN PUNCTURE WOUNDS... GIVE IT A FEW HOURS AND I'LL BE BACK IN THE FIGHT.

UHHNG... WHAT TIME IS IT?

EVENING OF THE 43RD, FOMAS. YOU'VE BEEN OUT MOST OF THE DAY.

SERGEANT, DID YOU FIND A GIRL'S BODY NEAR THE...?

SHE'S DOWN IN THE COOLER, FOMAS.

NOT A PRETTY SIGHT. YOUNG THING LIKE HER.

WHAT KIND OF BEAST'D CUT A GIRL UP LIKE THAT?

NOT NOW, SERGEANT. THE FIRE'S STOKING, AND WE'VE ALREADY LOST A DAY.

I NEED YOU TO GET THE RATS COMBAT-PREPPED...

FSSSH

FOMAS! GLAD TO SEE YOU'RE ALL RIGHT.

UH... CAPTAIN SHOYAN SENT ME TO TELL YOU THAT THE DREGUTAI--

--THE ARCHCOTARE THAT IS, NEEDS TO SEE YOU RIGHT AWAY.

ALL RIGHT, TELL 'EM I'LL BE UP AS SOON AS I CAN.

AND URCI...

I NEED YOUR MEN ASSEMBLED BY DAWN. THIS IS THE REAL THING.

YEAH, I FIGGERED ON IT, FOMAS. WE'LL BE READY.

BY ALL THE MARTYRS! WHAT DO YOU MEAN, BRINGING UNCLEAN FLESH INTO THIS HOLY SANCTUM?!

HOW DO YOU KNOW SHE'S UNCLEAN, DREGUS? HAVE YOU BEEN TALKING TO THE WHITE LOTUS YOURSELF LATELY?

THAT... THAT'S LIBEL!

SHUT UP AND LOOK AT THIS!

I TELL THEM EVERYTHING.

--THAT KESLING'S LOVER AND MURDERER WAS A VAYLEN.

--THAT A VAYLEN SLAVE SHIP IS UNDER GUARD IN THE CHOT HANGAR, AND THAT I'VE BEEN ABOARD IT... SEEN ITS HORRORS WITH MY OWN EYES.

--THAT THE LEADERS OF THE CHURCH OF THE TRANSITION, SOME OF THEM AT LEAST, ARE NO LONGER HUMAN.

THE DREGUTAI DON'T WANT TO HEAR IT. I WATCH THE STRUGGLE BEHIND THEIR FRIGHTENED EYES.

THEY'RE LOOKING FOR SOMETHING TO GRAB HOLD OF, TO PROVE THAT I'M A LYING TRAITOR.

BUT THEY CAN'T STOP STARING AT THE RAGGED WOUND IN DANNI'S NECK...

BERNEDOTH'S IDIOCY HAS BROUGHT US TO THIS...

I NEVER IMAGINED...

CERTAINLY, WE MUST TAKE IMMEDIATE ACTION. I SUGGEST WE HOLD A COUNCIL...

THERE'S NO TIME FOR THAT NOW! LAHK'S BLOOD! THE CHURCH OF THE TRANSITION IS A VAYLEN ENCLAVE. ALL OF HOTOK'S IN JEOPARDY!

I THINK WE'VE HEARD ENOUGH OF YOUR PROFANITIES, COTAR.

THIS IS A GRAVE MATTER, WHICH DESERVES THE UNDIVIDED ATTENTION OF THE DREGUTAI.

WE MUST HOLD A COUNCIL.

FINE. DO WHAT YOU LIKE.

I'M GOING TO SEE TO IT THIS GIRL GETS A PROPER CREMATION.

YOU WILL DO NOTHING OF THE KIND!

YOU'VE OVERSTEPPED YOUR AUTHORITY AND BROKEN IMPERIAL LAW ALREADY IN THIS MATTER.

CAPTAIN SHOYAN, COTAR-FOMAS FAITH IS BEING PLACED UNDER HOUSE ARREST. SEE TO IT THAT HE AND HIS MEN ARE ESCORTED AT ALL TIMES.

YES, YOUR HOLINESS.

CONFINE YOURSELF TO THE TEMPLE GROUNDS FOR THE PRESENT, COTAR-FOMAS--

--WE WILL HANDLE THIS CRISIS IN OUR OWN WAY.

CRAK

BLOODY COLD NIGHT.

DUNNO WHAT THE GRAND MASTER WAS THINKIN' WHEN HE CALLED A RETREAT THIS TIME 'A YEAR.

THEM FOOLS IS FREEZIN' THEIR NOODLES OFF DOWN THERE.

Tash

Tash

Tash

h

NO SWEAT, *SHOGUN*. DA SATCHEL CHARGE IST ON DA TOWAH.

I BROKE DA FUST GUARD'S NECK. DEY'LL TINK HE FELL UND KILT HIMSELF.

GOOD WORK, *GOPHER*.

RED TWO, HAVE YOU LOCATED THE GROUND LINE?

CHECK, RED LEADER. I'VE GOT A SOLID READING, CLOSE TO THE SURFACE.

I'LL BE READY FOR PICKUP IN TEN MINUTES.

TEN MINUTES, ROGER. RED LEADER OUT.

MARTYR'S WHEEL, WHAT DO THEY EXPECT ME TO DO?

LISTEN CAPTAIN, YOU PUT A COUPLE OF BOYS ON HIM, THEY KEEP WELL BACK. IF HE BOLTS, THEY LET HIM GO.

YOU'VE COVERED YOUR REAR, AND YOU HAVEN'T PISSED OFF THE FOMAS.

THEN YOU DO IT, GERNICK!

UH... I'M NOT REALLY THE RIGHT MAN FOR THE JOB, SIR.

THE FOMAS MIGHT BE INSULTED IF YOU SEND A JUNIOR GRADE OFFICER TO ARREST HIM...

LISTEN, THIS IS MADNESS. WE'RE SUPPOSED TO ARREST A MAN WHO HAS THE *GREY RATS* AS BODYGUARDS!

WHAT DO THEY EXPECT YOU TO DO? TAKE AN ENTIRE PLATOON TO HIS CHAMBERS?

WELL I'M NOT GOING. BE DAMNED IF I'M GOING TO BE REMEMBERED AS THE MAN WHO DIED TRYING TO ARREST HIS OWN FOMAS.

SORRY I'M LATE, CAPTAIN.

I'VE BEEN GETTIN' MY BOYS READY FOR THE FOMAS' NEXT BLEEDIN' LIVE-FIRE.

LIEUTENANT FOX! GOOD, GOOD. I'VE GOT A JOB FOR YOU.

TAKE TWO OF YOUR MEN, AND PLACE THE FOMAS UNDER HOUSE ARREST. ORDERS OF THE ARCH-COTARE.

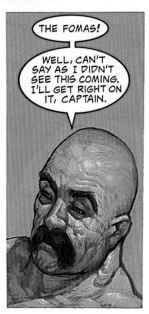

THE FOMAS!

WELL, CAN'T SAY AS I DIDN'T SEE THIS COMING. I'LL GET RIGHT ON IT, CAPTAIN.

COTAR-FOMAS? ARE YOU READY?

LET'S GO.

THEY'VE ORDERED YOUR ARREST SIR, LIKE YOU SAID THEY WOULD.

AND HERE YOU ARE.

YEAH... CAPTAIN SHOYAN WAS SWEATIN' LIKE A MAN WITH HIS HEAD ON THE BLOCK.

THIS IS THE RECON DATA YOU WANTED. IT'S BEEN DOWNLOADED INTO THE SLEDS ALREADY.

THESE CRYSTALS HERE ARE FOR YOUR IRON COMPUTERS.

ALL 'A THIRD COMPANY'S WITH YOU, FOMAS. THE BOYS ARE SCREWED UP TIGHTER 'N A KARSAN WHORE.

I'VE GOTTA TELL YOU, SIR, WE'VE BEEN WAITING FOR YOU FOR A LONG, LONG TIME...

FOX HAS DONE HIS WORK WELL.

FIVE BATTERED GIFV-350 *REVENGE* INFANTRY FIGHTING VEHICLES HOVER A HANDSBREADTH ABOVE THE PAVEMENT.

THE 350 IS BETTER ARMED THAN MOST TROOP-CARRIERS. ITS MAIN GUN IS THE F1605 *OSMAN* FUSOR. AN IMPERIAL COPY OF THE RENOWNED KARSAN GUN.

TWIN GATLING GUNS ON THE TURRET DECK ARE THE SHARP END OF A SOPHISTICATED POINT-DEFENSE SYSTEM THAT CAN DESTROY MISSILES AND ARTILLERY SHELLS IN FLIGHT.

HALBART'S AT THE DOOR WHEN WE SET DOWN. HE'S WHIP-TAUT, ANXIOUS TO GET ME IN IRON.

FOX'S EXECUTIVE OFFICER, SERGEANT MAJOR BORENSON, LOOKS NO LESS AGITATED.

LIEUTENANT, THE **SILVER ORCHID** HAS JUST RADIOED IN. THEY'VE RECEIVED THEIR LAUNCH CLEARANCE.

WHITE SECTION IS MOUNTED UP. THEY'RE WAITING FOR YOU.

NOTIFY **ORCHID** THAT WE'LL BE EMBARKING ON SCHEDULE, BORENSON.

FOMAS...

GOOD LUCK, SIR. I HOPE WE MEET AGAIN IN THE FLESH.

DO YOUR DUTY, LIEUTENANT, AND WE WILL.

WHITE ONE! THIS IS WHITE LEADER.

BUTTON 'ER UP, BOYS!

SINCE THE REST OF THE **RATS** ARE GEARED UP ALREADY, HALBART HAS CONSCRIPTED SERGEANT HOLBEIN'S STENTOR TO HELP ME INTO MY IRON.

THE EVEN, HEAVY PRESSURE OF THE ARMOR SURROUNDS ME AS THEY RUN IN THE SECURING BOLTS.

WE'LL BE SAFER ONCE WE'RE EN ROUTE. WHAT WE'RE PLANNING MUST BE INTERPRETED BY THE DREGUTAI AS TREASON.

BUT THE DREGUTAI ARE COMPLACENT IN THEIR AUTHORITY. THEY DON'T BELIEVE IN DISORDER.

THEY DON'T BELIEVE IN THE MONKEY-KING.

COMMANDER FIKE AND HIS IRON COMPANY HAVE JUST ARRIVED AT CAPITAL MAIN.

WITH THEIR LINE COMPANY TRAINING AT FORT GOLIN, THAT LEAVES ONE LINE COMPANY AND TWO PLATOONS OF IRON DEFENDING THE OBJECTIVE.

BUT THE MONKEY-KING IS **REAL**, AND HE'S KICKING DOWN THE GATES, AND THERE'S NO STOPPING HIM NOW.

I MOUNT UP WITH GREY ONE, HOLBEIN'S FIRE TEAM.

THE IFV'S TROOP COMPARTMENT IS BARELY LARGE ENOUGH TO HOLD SIX TROOPERS IN IRON.

THIS IS GREY LEADER. FORM UP ON GREY ONE IN GROUND EFFECT.

KEEP TO EXISTING ROADS AND MAINTAIN RADIO SILENCE UNTIL WE CROSS PHASE-LINE GOLD.

ROGER GREY LEADER.

ALL RIGHT, LET'S RIDE.

IF IT'S MONITORING THE AREA, THE CHOT'S SURVEILLANCE SATELLITE WILL IDENTIFY US AS NORMAL GROUND TRAFFIC.

--AND SINCE THE CHOT TEMPLE LIES NEAR A MAJOR TRUCKING ROAD, OUR APPROACH SHOULDN'T APPEAR SUSPICIOUS.

OF COURSE, IN A FEW MINUTES, THERE WON'T BE A CHOT SATELLITE TO WORRY ABOUT.

WE'RE ALL IN AGREEMENT THEN. THIS INFORMATION SHOULD BE BROUGHT TO THE ATTENTION OF THE LORD STEWARD.

I SUPPOSE IT MUST. I HOPE HE'S ASHAMED OF HIMSELF...RECKLESS YOUNG FOOL!

ON TO THE NEXT POINT THEN.

HOW DO WE REACH THE LORD STEWARD WITHOUT ALARMING THE HERETICS? THEY HAVE THE LORD STEWARD'S EAR...

WHEN WE CROSS ONTO ARTERIAL 10 NORTH, *GOREY* CLOSES THE SWITCH ON HER DETONATOR.

THE CHOT'S LOSCOM TOWER CRASHES FROM THE ROOF OF THE TEMPLE, ITS BASE SHATTERED BY *GOPHER'S* SATCHEL CHARGE.

B OOM

TEN KILOMETERS TO THE SOUTH, *GOREY'S* "CUTTER" GOES OFF--

SHOOF

--INCINERATING THE CHOT'S UNDERGROUND COMMUNICATIONS CABLE.

GREY LEADER TO SILVER ONE. ELIMINATE THE SATELLITE.

ACKNOWLEDGED.

GO AHEAD LOOP.

KAO KAO KAO

THE CHURCH OF THE TRANSITION HAS HAD ITS EYES GOUGED OUT. ITS TONGUE SLICED AWAY.

WHILE COMMANDER FIKE IS AT CAPITAL MAIN WITH THE TEMPLE'S IRON COMPANY--

MY *GREY RATS* ARE CLOSING IN FOR THE KILL.

GREY ONE AND GREY TWO BREAK OFF TO THE NORTH--

SSSSSHHHHH

--WHILE BORENSON'S SLEDS CONTINUE WEST ALONG THE GROUND ROAD.

SSSSSHHH

△ 104

HSR 1205

Arterial 10 North

△ 109

N`

△ 126

Black

Grey

HSR 208

AUSTA

△ 135

WHOOM
EEEEE

THEY DON'T HAVE A PRAYER.

EVEN 140 CM OF ENHANCED CERAMIC ARMOR CAN'T SHRUG OFF HITS FROM THE *REVENGE'S* MAIN GUN.

TAK
WHOOO
TAK TAK
TAK

SUN-BRIGHT BOLTS OF PLASMA IMPALE THE TOWERS. TURRETS LIFT INTO THE SKY ON PLUMES OF FIRE, THEIR READY STORES OF AMMUNITION FEEDING THE INFERNO.

ONCE THE HILL TOWERS ARE DOWN, WE RISE HIGHER STILL, SO THAT THE TEMPLE ITSELF IS UNMASKED.

THE TEMPLE'S DEFENSIVE GUNS SPIT TRACERS OUT OF THE VALLEY BEFORE EXPLODING, ONE AFTER ANOTHER, UNDER THE RAVENING HAMMER OF THE FUSORS.

GREY TWO TARGETS THE TEMPLE'S VEHICLE SHED WITH A SALVO OF ARMOR-PIERCING MISSILES.

HIGH-PRESSURE FUSION BOTTLES AND CHEMICAL FUEL STORES DO THE REST...

SSSSSSS

RIPPPPPPPRIP

I GIVE THE WORD, AND BLACK SECTION HEADS IN.

RIPPPP

CLANG

COTAR • FOMAS

CHAPTER 4: THE RIVER OF FIRE

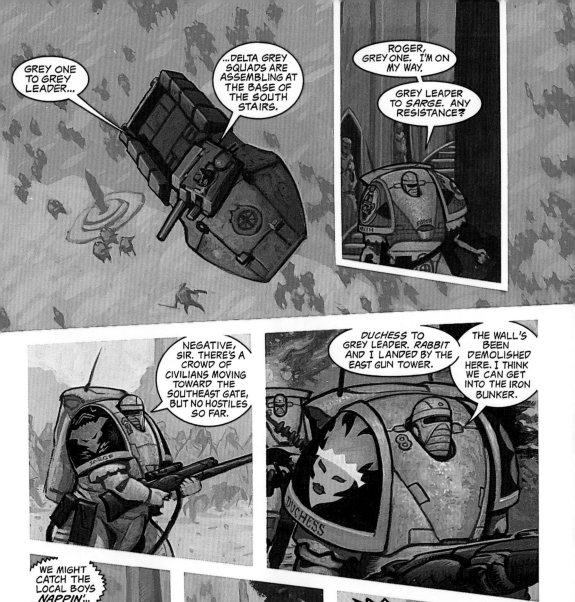

SSSSHAAA

ROGER, SHOGUN. I SEE IT!

THERE WAS *NOTHING* I COULD DO, YOUR EXCELLENCIES! THEY MUST HAVE PLANNED THIS OUT *CAREFULLY!*

LIEUTENANT FOX TOLD ME THAT HIS MEN WERE SIMPLY PREPARING FOR AN EXERCISE! IT WAS AN *ELABORATE* SCHEME...

ELABORATE SCHEME? YOU *IDIOT*, FAITH'S ONLY BEEN ON THE PLANET FOR EIGHT DAYS!

IF YOU DON'T BRING ME THIS TRAITOR IMMEDIATELY, I'LL *DRAG* YOU ONTO THE ROOF AND TIE YOU TO THE BURNING WHEEL *MYSELF!*

...EXCELLENCY...

GO YOU FOOL!

THERE SHE IS, LOOP. RIGHT ON SCHEDULE.

MERCATOR *SEGRELLES*, THIS IS THE *SILVER ORCHID*, REGISTRY HGS 3433. DROP YOUR DRIVES AND PREPARE TO RECEIVE AN INSPECTION PARTY.

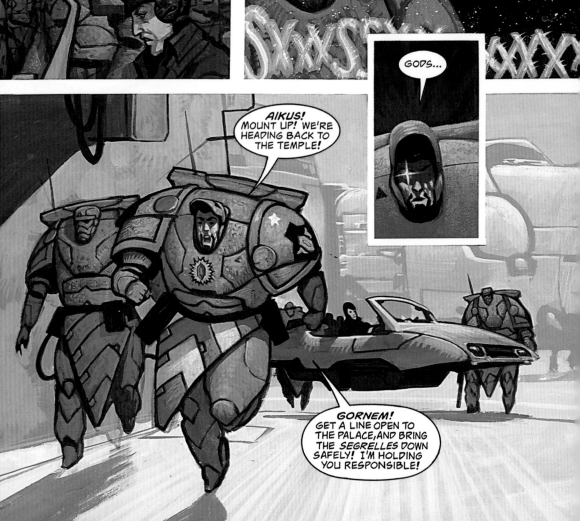

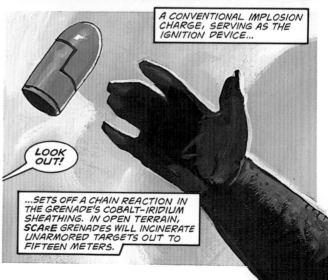

IN A CONFINED BUNKER LIKE THIS ONE...

BWOOM

FIRE IN THE HOLE, DUCHESS!

CAUGHT 'EM NAPPIN', NO QUESTION ABOUT IT!

DUCHESS TO GREY LEADER. WE NAILED THE BUNKER. I THINK WE GOT 'EM ALL, BUT WE'RE GONNA GO IN AND SECURE IT.

ROGER, DUCHESS. BE CAREFUL!

OUR MOUNTS HAVE GONE SOUTH TO SCREEN THE STARPORT, AND WE'RE TAKING SMALL-ARMS FIRE FROM INSIDE THE TEMPLE.

I'D ESTIMATE ONE PLATOON TO A COMPANY. WE CAN'T ACHIEVE FIRE SUPERIORITY FROM OUR POSITION HERE...

WHUMP

GREY LEADER, THIS IS BLACK LEADER. WE'VE REACHED THE TRUCK PARK AND ARE ADVANCING ON THE TEMPLE.

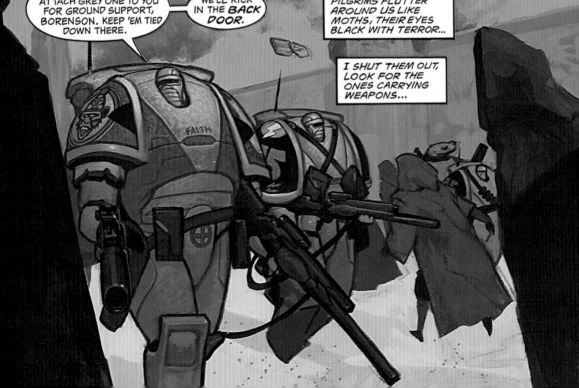

I'M GOING TO CROSS-ATTACH GREY ONE TO YOU FOR GROUND SUPPORT, BORENSON. KEEP 'EM TIED DOWN THERE.

WE'LL KICK IN THE BACK DOOR.

PILGRIMS FLUTTER AROUND US LIKE MOTHS, THEIR EYES BLACK WITH TERROR...

I SHUT THEM OUT, LOOK FOR THE ONES CARRYING WEAPONS...

FAITH

I DON'T HAVE LONG TO WAIT.

KSSHHH

I'M HIT!

TAR-BABY, WALK YOUR FUSOR ALONG THE CLOISTERS! THEY'RE IN THE CLOISTERS!

SHOGUN, YOU ALL RIGHT?

UHH... YEAH. MY SHOULDER'S NUMB, BUT THE DRUGS'RE KICKIN' IN.

I'M ALL RIGHT.

GO FOR THE MAIN DOORS! GOPHER, WATCH THE WEST CLOISTERS FOR A CROSSFIRE!

I'M RIGHT ABOUT THE CROSSFIRE.

THEY'VE WAITED FOR US TO GET WITHIN SPITTING RANGE OF THEIR GRENADE LAUNCHERS.

RRAAAGH!

PUNT

SSSSSSSSS

EEAAKH!

WHUMP

KRACK
KRACK
WOO-HOO!
THAT'S IT, BABY! SHE AIN'T MOVIN' OR SHOOTIN' AGAIN THIS SIDE OF A DRY DOCK!
THE TARGET'S BEEN NEUTRALIZED, LIEUTENANT. SEND YOUR MEN ACROSS.
GOOD LUCK.
YOU HEARD THE LADY!
MOVE IT OUT!

THIS IS IT.

GOREY, CHECK THE ENTIRE ROOM FOR SIGNATURES LIKE THOSE WE FOUND ON THE *GISELLE.*

YESSIR.

LOOKS MORE LIKE AN *ASSEMBLY LINE* THAN A HOSPITAL TO ME, FOMAS...

SHOGUN, TAKE YOUR TEAM OUT AND WATCH THE CORRIDOR.

THE REST OF YOU STAY SHARP FOR BOOBY TRAPS...

GOT IT! BEHIND THE WEST WALL!

THERE'S A MEDIUM-SIZED CHAMBER THAT'S BEEN SEALED UP. NO DOOR.

BLOW IT OPEN, GOREY.

FOMAS, WE'VE GOT MOVEMENT DOWN AROUND THE MAIN JUNCTION...

DON'T LET ANY HOSTILES THROUGH, SHOGUN.

ALL THE SAME GEAR AS THE *GISELLE,* FOMAS...

PROBES, HOLDING TANKS, AND DRAWERS FULL OF THESE HULLING KNIVES.

NO WORMS, THOUGH...

AAAUGH!

WE GOT *ACTION,* FOMAS!

KREEEE

BRAP-P

SARGE, GET OUT THERE AND BACK UP SHOGUN'S TEAM--

GOREY, MAKE A VISUAL RECORD OF THAT CHAMBER, AND GET OVER HERE BESIDE ME.

LET'S TAKE THIS PLACE APART.

AMEN.

POOM·POOM·POOM·POOM

WHAT'S THE SITUATION OUT HERE?

NOTHIN' NOW, FOMAS.

TWO SQUADS OF SKINS MADE A SUICIDE CHARGE. THEY DIDN'T HAVE A CHANCE.

WE'VE CHECKED A GOOD HALF-DOZEN BODIES, AND NONE OF 'EM WERE HULLED.

FIKE COULDN'T DRAG HIS WHOLE BATTALION OUT TO THE STARPORT, DING.

THAT'S WHAT THE HOSPITAL WAS FOR.

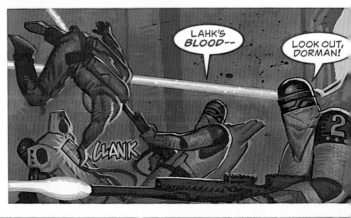

"WE'LL HAVE A BLEEDIN' FISH FRY TONIGHT, WON'T WE, CAPTAIN?"

Tash   Tash

DEPLOY IN LINE. FIVE METERS BETWEEN EACH OF YOU!

DON'T **BUNCH UP!**

IT IS THE THUNDER OF THE BURNING WHEEL THAT YOU HEAR BEHIND YOU--

Tash

--THE HOT BREATH OF THE SECRET FIRE THAT BURNS ALL ABOUT YOU!

I'VE GOT YOU NOW, YOU ARROGANT BASTARD...

FLEE THIS DEN OF DESTROYERS! YOUR IMMORTAL SOULS ARE IN PERIL HERE!

KREEEEE

KSHHHH

I DON'T HAVE A CHANCE OF DRAWING ON HIM.

FOMAS!

BUT THAT DOESN'T MATTER.

FOMAS...

S-STILL HERE, SARGE...

PAIN SURGES OUT FROM MY CHEST IN A CRIMSON JET.

THERE'S A SHARP HISS AS THE IRON FLOODS ME WITH FOAM, AND THEN I DON'T FEEL ANYTHING.

MERISSA WAS RIGHT...

...MY FATHER'S HANDS DRAG ME OUT OF A RED SEA OF AGONY...

...AND INTO THE DARK.

THE LORD-STEWARD'S PALACE, TWO DAYS LATER.

YOUR HEARING IS OVER, COTAR-FOMAS.

THE PEERS HAVE HEARD YOUR EVIDENCE.

THIS REQUEST FOR A PRIVATE HEARING WILL DO YOU NO GOOD.

YOUR RELIGION IS NOT WELCOME IN THE EMPIRE. IT VIES WITH THE EMPEROR FOR THE HEARTS AND SOULS OF HIS SUBJECTS.

AND IN THAT CONTEST THERE CAN ONLY BE ONE WINNER.

CUT THE CRAP.

YOU KNOW WE'VE GOT YOU BY THE THROAT, OR YOU WOULDN'T HAVE GRANTED US THIS HEARING.

HERE ARE OUR DEMANDS.

WHAT DEMANDS!?

YOUR FOLLY NEEDN'T BE MADE PUBLIC, BARON.

THE PEOPLE NEED NEVER KNOW THAT YOU WERE PROTECTING A VAYLEN ENCLAVE ON HOTOK... THAT YOU WERE INTENDING TO PLACE A VAYLEN UNIT INSIDE THE KEEP.

TAK

THEY WILL ONLY KNOW WHAT WAS MADE PUBLIC DURING THE HEARING THIS MORNING... THAT THE CHURCH CRUSHED A DANGEROUS AND HERETICAL CULT.

THINK ABOUT IT, BERNEDOTH.

"A MAN WITH A SENSIBLE NATURE FINDS THAT FATE ROLLS WITH HIM."

YOUR LORDSHIP! PLEASE EXCUSE THE RASH WORDS OF THIS...

GAKK!

THAT'S THE LAST TIME YOU INTERRUPT ME, YOU STINKING RAT!

THE PROPHET AHMILAHK CALLED *FREE WILL* AN ILLUSION, A CLOAK OF STONE DRAPED OVER THE SHOULDERS OF A CHILD.

ONLY WHEN FATE'S BLACK FIST SMASHES THE CLOAK, CAN THE ETERNAL FLAME RISE FREE, TO DANCE BEFORE THE BREATH OF DESTINY.

WHEN MY SOLID LIFE WAS SHATTERED, I TOOK A NEW NAME.

I LEFT MY WIFE, MY CHILD, AND MY HOME AND ENTERED THE RIVER OF FIRE.

TAP

I HAVE NO GUIDE NOW, SAVE INSTINCT. MINE IS A FLOATING WORLD. NO FOUNDATION. NOTHING TO STAND ON.

YET MY WARRIORS TRAIL AFTER ME, CLINGING TO MY BACK, INTO DEATH AND RUIN...

THIS A PRIVATE PARTY?

I SAW YOU AT THE PYRES. THOUGHT YOU MIGHT WANT TO TALK TO SOMEBODY AFTERWARD.

I'VE BEEN TO MY SHARE OF PYRES, GEIL. IT COMES WITH THE TERRITORY.

I WONDER HOW MANY ARE BURNING AT THE CHURCH OF THE TRANSITION TONIGHT?

WE KILLED AT LEAST FIFTY OF THEIR SOLDIERS IN THE RAID. MOST OF THEM DIED THINKING THEY WERE DEFENDING SOMETHING WORTHWHILE.

THAT'S TRUE.

ON THE OTHER HAND... THERE ARE ABOUT TWENTY MILLION PEOPLE WHO OWE YOU THEIR LIVES TONIGHT.

HAVE YOU GOT A CIGARETTE?

SURE.

THANKS.

I WONDER IF YOU KNOW JUST HOW MANY DOORS YOU'VE KICKED IN AROUND HERE, FAITH.

YOU'VE MADE MORE ENEMIES IN A WEEK THAN OLD COGITO MADE IN SIXTY YEARS.

OF COURSE, YOU'VE MADE FOLLOWERS, TOO. YOU'VE GOT THIS TEMPLE EATING OUT OF YOUR HAND.

TSST

AS A RAVILAR, I CAN'T COMPLAIN. IT'S A HELL OF A STORY.

BUT YOU'RE HEADING DOWN A DANGEROUS PATH, TREVOR, AND THERE'S A LOT AT STAKE...

IT'S THE ONLY *REAL* PATH, GEIL.

THE RIVER OF FIRE...

...EVERYTHING ELSE IS AN ILLUSION.

COTAR • FOMAS

THE GREY RATS

IN HONOR OF OUR **488** KICKSTARTER SUPPORTERS, WITHOUT WHOM, THIS BOOK WOULD NOT HAVE BEEN POSSIBLE.

PRAISE AHMILAHK.

GREY RATS HONOR GUARD, MOSUM TO HOTOK

THE ORIGINAL GREY RATS HONOR GUARD (IRON), MOSUM

	Iron #
Client Cotar-Fomas Trevor Faith	1
Squad Leader Jasek "Sarge" Holbein	2
Asst. Squad Leader Maurice "Shogun" Kakuda	3
LAS-50 Laser Rifle Cozi "Gorey" Togoro	4
LAS-50 Laser Rifle Grace "Tar-Baby" Tarmina	5
LAS-50 Laser Rifle Tash "Rabbit" Mitsubo	6
LAS-50 Laser Rifle Oskor "Retch" Vincasa	7
Kharkar FA75 Fusor Support Trace "Duchess" Varik	8
Kharkar FA75 Fusor Support K'ofir "Gopher"	9
Commo Shucka "Ding" Benthabi	10
Medic Shamine "Doc" Alshift (KIA)	11

THE GREY RATS GUARDS PLATOON (IRON), HOTOK

PLATOON HQ

Platoon Leader Jasek "Sarge" Holbein	2
Platoon Maurice "Shogun" Kakuda	3
FOC/Forward Observer V.K. "Snapper" Friedrich	18
Communications Shucka "Ding" Benthabi	10
Medic Lee "Leech" O'Connor	19

SQUAD A

	Iron #
Team Leader Grace "Tar-Baby" Tarmina	5
Kharkar FA75 Fusor Support Trace "Duchess" Varik	8
LAS-50 Laser Rifle Adam "Long Knife" Duncan	7
LAS-50 Laser Rifle Kristin "Princess" Hayworth	12
LAS-50 Laser Rifle Ankaris "Big Thirteen"	13
LAS-50 Laser Rifle James A. "Scavenger" Wu	14
LAS-50 Laser Rifle Wexer "Wax Off"	15
LAS-50 Laser Rifle Jeff "Shark Bite"	16
Medic Shervyn Van "Bones"	17

SQUAD B

Group Leader Cozi "Gorey" Togoro	4
Kharkar FA75 Fusor Support Chris "Hambone" Allingham	20
LAS-50 Laser Rifle Jonathan "Cutter" Czisny	21
LAS-50 Laser Rifle Red "6" Fuji	22
LAS-50 Laser Rifle Mike "Bomber" Bawden	23
LAS-50 Laser Rifle Colin "Archer" Booth	24
LAS-50 Laser Rifle Wilhelm "Pres" Fitzpatrick	25
LAS-50 Laser Rifle James Edward "The Duke" Reed	26
Medic Dominic "Nikko" de Borja	27

SQUAD C

Group Leader Tash "Rabbit" Mitsubo	6
Kharkar FA75 Fusor Support Oskor "Retch" Vincasa	7
LAS-50 Laser Rifle Robert "Desslok" Doherty	30
LAS-50 Laser Rifle Eric "Fighter" Mersmann	31
LAS-50 Laser Rifle John "Overwatch" Machin	32
LAS-50 Laser Rifle Michael Wm "Dauntless" Kaluta	33
LAS-50 Laser Rifle Daniel "Battle Tank" Abram	34
LAS-50 Laser Rifle Derek "Brother" Grimm	35
Medic Bryce "Sawbones"	36

ASSAULT TEAM

Kharkar FA75 Fusor Support K'ofir "Gopher"	9
Kharkar FA75 Fusor Support Jay "Terrier" Russell	40
Iron Assault Trooper Radek "Oro" Drozdalski	41
Iron Assault Trooper Kevin J. "Lighthorse" Lee	42
Iron Assault Trooper Aaron "Kaiser" Tobul	43
Iron Assault Trooper Wijse "Eagle Eye"	44

HOTOK TEMPLE GUARD

MUNDUS HUMANITAS TEMPLE GUARD BATTALION, HOTOK

THE OLD GUARD

BATTALION HEADQUARTERS

Bttn Commander Cotar-Fomas Trevor Faith
Bttn XO Captain Eria Shoyan
Personnel Ofc. Peter North
Intel Ofc. Jeffrey Yandora
Operations Ofc. Ron Jeremy
Quartermaster Hochlin Semmins
Bttn. FOC Fabio Torquin
HQ Aide de Camp Brett Bather
TOC Aide de Camp Ted Lepe
TOC Aide de Camp Victor Cervantes

BATTALION VEHICLES

#00 GTOC Commander Mark Mazz
Gunner Raymond Costries
Pilot Naomi Beck
Tac. Operations Spec Douglas Alan Markwell
#01 Commander Scott Fountain
Gunner Mike Kim
#02 Commander Christopher Beck
Gunner Har Donn

1ST COMPANY (IRON)

COMPANY HEADQUARTERS

COMPANY HQ TEAM

Company Commander Tomas Gernick
Senior NCO Frank Zamorano
Forward Observer Richard "Boomer" Camacho
Co. FOC Cynthia "Scope" Rivera
Gunner Daniel "Walker" Walker
Gunner Richard "Teach" Javitt
Security Tony "Carver" Valenti
Communications Cristobal "Zapper" Ibarra

HEADQUARTERS VEHICLES

#10 GTOC Commander Cmdr. Alice M. Ivey
    Gunner Charles Zagami
    Pilot Matt Gramum
#11 Commander Joseph C. Eck
    Gunner Luis E. Castro
    Pilot Desi A. Escabi

1ST PLATOON (IRON)

Platoon Leader "Victor" Victoria
Platoon Sergeant "Dragon" Itelli
Medic Florencio "Doc" Lim
Communications Jay "Sparks" Man
Support Weapon Black Dragon
Support Weapon Lee "Striker" Streicher
Support Weapon Chris "Hammer" Falls
Support Weapon Nicole "Ace" Falls
Forward Observer Idalia "Toaster" Robinson
F/O Commo Allan "Ringer" Gallardo

1ST SQUAD: STORM RIDERS

Squad Leader Greg "Rider" Dalpe
Assistant Squad Leader
    Dean "Shredder" Shimonishi
Rifleman Gerimi "Burly" Burleight
Rifleman Steven "Red Rider" Redd
Rifleman Jon "The Butcher" Metzger
Rifleman Russell "Ripper" Vanderhue
Rifleman Andrew "Monster" Trowbridge
Rifleman Andrea "Belle" Bixby
Support Weapon Ken "The Beast" Hamlin
Support Weapon Andy H "Blaster" Chang

2ND SQUAD: PROPHET'S FIST

Squad Leader Lars "Fist" Nielson
Assistant Squad Leader
    Armiger Pilot John "Mega" Degaitas
Rifleman Justin "Pretty Boy" Vargas
Rifleman Ron "Stone Man" glass
Rifleman Joon "Slasher" Hyon
Rifleman Phixay "Snake" Phavong
Rifleman Ron "Marksman" Marz
Rifleman Paul "Heartbreaker" Guinan
Support Weapon Cully "Hammer" Hamner
Support Weapon James "Rubberhead" Robinson

3RD SQUAD: FIRE LIONS

Squad Leader Dave "Rolling Thunder" Dorman
Assistant Squad Leader Dave "Big Gun" Johnson
Rifleman Geoff "Nixon" Darrow
Rifleman Jerry "Tattoo" Prosser
Rifleman T.Y. "Low Rider" Loh
Rifleman John "Bad Boy" McMillan
Rifleman Nathan "Shark Bait" Hyde
Rifleman Dan "Frosty" Frazee
Support Weapon Pietro "Scorcher" La Grece
Support Weapon Trevor "Goshawk" Rodger

1ST PLATOON VEHICLES

#110 Commander Mike Jaramillo
    Gunner Dan Robers
    Pilot Dan Dacier
#111 Commander Kevan Ulsaler
    Gunner Oylan Cole
    Pilot Donne E. Johnson
#112 Commander Joe Butler
    Gunner Mark Aviles
    Pilot Dennis Canel
#113 Commander Brent Goodman
    Gunner Johnathan Wright
    Pilot Jim Mason

2ND PLATOON (IRON)

Platoon Leader R.J. "King" Spassov
Platoon Sergeant Hiram "Gunmaster" Hong
Medic Michael "Grunt" Gruden
Communications Ryan "Ding" James
Support Weapon Chris "Gaffer" Gruden
Support Weapon Robert "Hacker" Cardoso
Support Weapon Eric "Armageddon" Arrfaga
Support Weapon Richardo "Street" Colon
Forward Observer Stevie "Hawkeye" Carrillo
F/O Commo Gabriel "Angel" Vega

HOTOK TEMPLE GUARD

1ST SQUAD: VOID HAWKS

Squad Leader Cozi "Lizard Liver" Shawndoo
Assistant Squad Leader Antonio "Fish" Farina
Rifleman Vince "Charger" Carrillo
Rifleman Brian "Bruiser"
Rifleman Kelly "Cruiser"
Rifleman George L. "Laughing Boy" Kohn
Rifleman Nickolas B. "Battleaxe" Kohn
Rifleman Mike "Massacre" Mitchell
Support Weapon Cesar "Emperor" Esquer
Support Weapon Edward "Road Kill" Rodela

2ND SQUAD: IRON SCOURGE

Squad Leader Darren "Scourge" Escobedo
Assistant Squad Leader Bryan "Devil" Koester
Rifleman Raymond "Butcher" Elliot
Rifleman John "War Born" Takei
Rifleman Chick "Stumpy" Earthmage
Rifleman Chris "Master" Cousinequ
Rifleman Don "Thrasher" Goss
Rifleman Moes "Mole Man" Cardosso
Support Weapon Rick "Bullet" Kovacs
Support Weapon John "Bullroarer" Fudlas

3RD SQUAD: PROPHET'S SONS

Squad Leader Kent "Sonny" Johnson
Assistant Squad Leader James "Laser" Walker II
Rifleman Wayne A. "Bullwhip" Wong
Rifleman Riki "Savage" Ozaki
Rifleman Joshua "Blood"
Rifleman Mark "Rattler" Finn
Rifleman Mike "Death" Clark
Rifleman Neil "Ike" Englehart
Support Weapon Susan "Wild Girl" Gallagher
Support Weapon Alaiyo "Scrapper" Bradshaw

2ND PLATOON VEHICLES

#120 Commander Dennis Wnthen
    Gunner Bill Nahey
    Pilot Nguyen Dong
#121 Commander Austin Ripley
    Gunner Jonathan Froines
    Pilot Justin Wieland
#122 Commander Andy Nash
    Gunner Dave Yu
    Pilot Bill Johnson
#123 Commander Michael Favila
    Gunner Virginia Marfori
    Pilot Simon Clustin

3RD PLATOON (IRON)

Platoon Leader Mark "Buff" Applebaum
Platoon Sergeant John "Lancer" Dirito
Medic Anne "Scalpel" Looseman
Communications Kevin "Buzz" Moeller
Support Weapon Chris "Thumper" Morris
Support Weapon Diz "Rhino" Davis
Support Weapon C.J. "Battleship" Wostal
Forward Observer Ivan "Groucho" Hicks
F/O Commo Ryan "Top Net" Alvarez

1ST SQUAD: SPIRIT'S FLAIL

Squad Leader Dawn "Ibn" Moeller
Assistant Squad Leader
    Rosendo "Quicksilver" Alazar
Rifleman Howard "Crusher" Boyd
Rifleman Arlyn "Speed" Pillay
Rifleman Derek "Bad Blood" Thompson
Rifleman Jason "Predator" Uerkvitz
Rifleman Jesse "Stalker" Munch
Rifleman Steven "War God" Voight
Support Weapon Alan "Harlequin" Sinder
Support Weapon James "Shock" Little

2ND SQUAD: DREADNOUGHTS

Squad Leader Jonathan "Dreadnought" Grace
Assistant Squad Leader
    Junior Scott M. "Black Skull" Gilmore
Rifleman Caleb "Demon" Ruggiero
Rifleman Ryan "Chucker" Graff
Rifleman Jeremy "Vulcan" Alires
Rifleman Erik "Sabre" Uisaker
Rifleman Polo "Demolisher" Chavez
Rifleman Alfredo "Cthulu" Yruretagoyena
Support Weapon Andrew "Mecha" Mannion
Support Weapon Don "Whipsaw" Walker

3RD SQUAD: IRON DIAMONDS

Squad Leader James "Diamond" Sinbury
Assistant Squad Leader
    Dwayne "Chain Gang" Wilson
Rifleman Jefrey "Pistol" Koga
Rifleman Ian "Legend" McIntosh
Rifleman Nolan Pascal "Shaver" Pillay
Rifleman Paola "Vandal" Gonzalez
Rifleman Carlos H. "Horse" Hernandez
Rifleman Barb "Wire" Rothacher
Support Weapon Jeff "Hi" Keeran
Support Weapon Mekron "HI Mom" Heard

3RD PLATOON VEHICLES

#130 Commander John R. Byrd
    Gunner Ken McGehee
    Pilot James Lee
#131 Commander Jeremy Radisich
    Gunner Brandon Trapse
    Pilot Matthew Ibarra
#132 Commander Ben Tobey
    Gunner Vinton Houch
    Pilot Josh Tobey
#133 Commander Daniel Bethal
    Gunner Albert Salvato
    Pilot Wayne West

2

2ND COMPANY (ANVIL)

HEADQUARTERS PLATOON

COMPANY HQ TEAM

Company Commander Siever Ovis
Senior NCO Rick Tucker
Forward Observer Elliot Blake
Co. FOC Michael Stradford
Gunner Dean Harvey
Gunner Baine Jung
Security S.H. Rizor
Communications Eddro Rivas

HEADQUARTERS VEHICLES

#20 GTOC Commander Benjamin Davis
    Gunner David A. Dribbin
    Pilot David Huerta
#21 Commander Chris W. Henry
    Gunner Lance Wm. Karutz
    Pilot Matt Valdivina

1ST PLATOON (ANVIL)

Platoon Leader Ruben Sears
Platoon Sergeant Salvador Leon
Medic Juan Carlos
Communications Geoff Scott
Support Weapon Jim Shull
Support Weapon Andrew Wolffe
Support Weapon Octavio Islas
Support Weapon Jonathan M. Plotz
Forward Observer Richelle Marfori
F/O Commo Doug Snyder

HOTOK TEMPLE GUARD

1ST SQUAD: MIGHTY ANVIL

Squad Leader Benito Santiago
Assistant Squad Leader Francis Avecilla
Rifleman Juan F. Muro
Rifleman David Green
Rifleman Charles Paul
Rifleman Nathan Green
Rifleman Tom Masante
Rifleman Steve Kim
Support Weapon Alex Vara De Rey
Support Weapon Jason Felix

2ND SQUAD: SILVER KNIVES

Squad Leader Richard Jaritt
Assistant Squad Leader Damon Gregory
Rifleman Tracy Miller
Rifleman Theordore J. Jons
Rifleman Sherry Magpali
Rifleman Jeff Fennel
Rifleman Tim M. Peters
Rifleman Mark T. Price
Support Weapon Sean Chumbley
Support Weapon Gereard D. Harp

3RD SQUAD: TALONS

Squad Leader John Alley
Assistant Squad Leader L. Keenan Mills
Rifleman Steve Kramer
Rifleman Richard Bard
Rifleman Michael Lupez
Rifleman Garrett Trotter
Rifleman Chris Martin
Rifleman Jackson "Action"
Support Weapon Elliot Kunde
Support Weapon Dustin Clayton

1ST PLATOON VEHICLES

#210 Commander Pannel Vaughn
    Gunner Jim A. Clark
    Pilot Lisa Hechtmach
#211 Commander Marcus A. Bonilla
    Gunner Jim Edquilang
    Pilot Jason Spears
#212 Commander Robby Sison
    Gunner Adrian Nerida
    Pilot Jaheeli Garnett
#213 Commander Chris LeFall
    Gunner David K. Wong
    Pilot Harold Manly

2ND PLATOON (ANVIL)

Platoon Leader Larry Willis
Platoon Sergeant Gerry Salas
Medic Sawyer Frugé
Communications Jeremy Hammer
Support Weapon James Nunn
Support Weapon Gary Deocampo
Support Weapon Alonzo Martinez
Support Weapon C. McLaughlin
Forward Observer Tell Lynn
F/O Commo Peter Yeung

1ST SQUAD: THRASHERS

Squad Leader Jake Macholtz
Assistant Squad Leader John Koger
Rifleman Roger Robinson
Rifleman Stephanie Falls
Rifleman Brad Markey
Rifleman Peter Tsai
Rifleman Alicia Swan
Rifleman Bob Eames
Support Weapon Colin Ruie
Support Weapon Jack Haden

2ND SQUAD: PROPHET'S AVENGERS

Squad Leader Joseph Calderon
Rifleman Squad Leader L. J. Kerr
Rifleman John Weas
Rifleman Carl Frank
Rifleman Joey Lindquist
Rifleman Steve Michalek
Rifleman Kofi Arhin
Rifleman Daniel Jackson
Support Weapon Josh Grey
Support Weapon Richard Lee

3RD SQUAD: FIRE EAGLES

Squad Leader Sterling Jones
Assistant Squad Leader G.G. Dean, Jr.
Rifleman Ernest Sanchez
Rifleman Morris Kakuda
Rifleman Patrick Pearlman
Rifleman Frederick Eirich
Rifleman Maria Dehne
Rifleman Donna Beames
Support Weapon Rob McDaniel
Support Weapon Brian McDaniel

2ND PLATOON VEHICLES

#220 Commander Justin McDaniel
    Gunner Rudy Vazmina
    Pilot Allison Beames
#221 Commander Lauren Beames
    Gunner Ernest Di Pietro
    Pilot Jeffery Kidd
#222 Commander Kurt Mericli
    Gunner Chris Russell
    Pilot Bob Rose
#223 Commander Ursula Eirich
    Gunner Fenton Glover
    Pilot Susan Dehne

3RD PLATOON (ANVIL)
THE YOUNG GUARD

Platoon Leader Johannes av Esternvaille
Platoon Sergeant Eloy Cintron
Medic Eric Franklin
Communications Jack Gulick
Support Weapon Jason MacGillivray
Support Weapon Ville Ojanperä
Support Weapon Chris McEligot
Support Weapon Sam Tlustos
Forward Observer Helder Lavigne
F/O Commo. Commo Rich Thomas

1ST SQUAD: FIRE WALKERS

Squad Leader T M Romanelli
Assistant Squad Leader L. Kevin Weiser
Rifleman Sim Page
Rifleman George Panopoulos
Rifleman Jesse "Vega"
Rifleman Gare Reeve
Rifleman Nathan 'Noofy' Roberts
Rifleman Race DiLoreto
Support Weapon Tom "Big Brother"
Support Weapon Jason C Jones

2ND SQUAD: BLACK DRAGONS

Squad Leader P.J. Crader
Assistant Squad Leader L. Andrew Lohmann
Rifleman Scott Maynard
Rifleman Joseph "Emperor"
Rifleman Revek "The Gorgon"
Rifleman Yoshi "Sniper"
Rifleman Jason "Halloween"
Rifleman Martin Liven
Support Weapon Joe Greathead
Support Weapon William Lee

HOTOK TEMPLE GUARD

3RD SQUAD: VULCANS

Squad Leader Norb "Muskox"
Assistant Squad Leader Ilan Muskat
Rifleman Juliusz "Caesar"
Rifleman Marius Blascheck
Rifleman Chip and Erin
Rifleman Josh Mrazek
Rifleman Erik Augustsson
Rifleman Richard Nichols
Support Weapon Kenneth Fjelleng
Support Weapon Ray "Fusor"

3RD PLATOON VEHICLES

#230 Commander Michael "Bowtie" Muske
   Gunner David Tai
   Pilot Donald R. Edwards
#231 Commander Dominic Duggan
   Gunner Scott Forgue
   Pilot Daniel Camozzato
#232 Commander Judd Karlman
   Gunner Beorn Elieser Jonsson
   Pilot C.L. McCartney
#233 Commander Steve Moore
   Gunner Liam Seven Five Double-O Five
   Pilot Anthony Hanlon

3RD COMPANY (ANVIL)

HEADQUARTERS PLATOON

COMPANY HQ TEAM

Company Commander Baroni "Old Man"
Senior NCO Tim "Buzz" Isakson
Forward Observer Sgt. Dan Gibson
Co. FOC Mark Newman
Gunner Bill Kraut
Gunner Christian Hübinger
Security Daniel Rodriguez
Communications Rick Tucker

HEADQUARTERS VEHICLES

#20 GTOC Commander John Tipton
   Gunner Quek JiaJin
   Pilot Nicholas
#21 Commander Walt Larson
   Gunner Hamish Mabon-Ross
   Pilot Tony "The Tiger"

1ST PLATOON (ANVIL)

Platoon Leader Marios Poulimenos
Platoon Sergeant Anthony Hersey
Medic Alberto Casu
Communications Drumms "Balrog"
Support Weapon Jonathan Wooley
Support Weapon Sam Slocum
Support Weapon Bruce Turner
Support Weapon James "Taurus"
Support Weapon Paul N "Specs"
Support Weapon John Bogart

1ST SQUAD: MIGHTY ANVIL

Squad Leader Jeremy Mohler
Assistant Squad Leader Gersch "Big Boss"
Rifleman David E Nebiker
Rifleman Arthur William Breon III
Rifleman Midhun Mathew
Rifleman Brad "Bullroarer"
Support Weapon Guy MacDonnell
Support Weapon Todd Grotenhuis

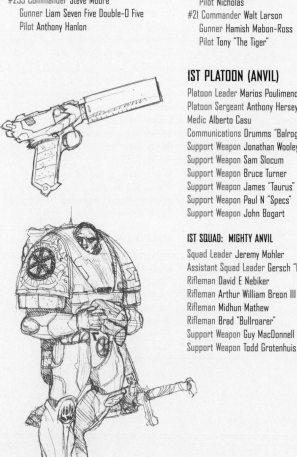

Support Weapon Gunnar Bangsmoen
Support Weapon Parker D Hicks
Forward Observer Olivier von Seelow
F/O Commo Kayne Newell

1ST SQUAD: THRASHERS

Squad Leader Stras "Old Captain"
Assistant Squad Leader John Roberts
Rifleman Dudley "Number Ten"
Rifleman Adriano Antonini
Rifleman Chris Casman
Rifleman Alex "The Grumbler"
Rifleman Nathan "Slayer"
Rifleman Jonas Vulgrim
Support Weapon John "Longshot"
Support Weapon D. Hoffmann

2ND SQUAD: PROPHET'S AVENGERS

Squad Leader Matt "Disco" Erickson
Assistant Squad Leader Justin "Watchman"
Rifleman Rich Koenig
Rifleman Dal "The Destroyer"
Rifleman Brendan G Conway
Rifleman Adam "Firstborn"
Rifleman Craig Maloney
Rifleman Jeff Russell
Support Weapon Simon D. Bergeron
Support Weapon Rich "Indie"

3RD SQUAD: FIRE EAGLES

Squad Leader Exarch
Assistant Squad Leader Derek Guder
Rifleman Michael Nielsen
Rifleman Morgan Ellis
Rifleman Hundmathr
Rifleman Samuel Gordon Mitson
Rifleman Dan Zelman
Rifleman Mike "New Kid"
Support Weapon Ray Powell
Support Weapon Kevin Kauffman

2ND PLATOON VEHICLES

#320 Commander Thelonicon
   Gunner Xn Mojo
   Pilot Goran "Thrillrider"
#321 Commander Mark Argent
   Gunner Jason O' Mahony
   Pilot Inannipal "Fletcher"
#322 Commander John Trudgian
   Gunner Rob B. "The Donk" Donkin
   Pilot Christine Chen
#323 Commander William Goodspeed
   Gunner Saddock
   Pilot K'uphir Vaas

CHURCH OF THE TRANSITION

3RD MONASTIC SHOCK RIFLE COMPANY, CHURCH OF THE TRANSITION, HOTOK

COMPANY HEADQUARTERS

Company Commander Victorious Germanicus
Company Executive Officer Albert Andersen
    Headquarters Staff Zed Lopez
    Headquarters Staff John Kane
    Headquarters Staff Jeff Cross
Medic Kurt Franks
Gunner with KVSG Machinegun Scott Early
    Assistant Gunner Blair Nicholson
Company Adjutant Vidal Bairos

COMPANY A-7 LASER PLATOON (A-7 LASER)

Section One Leader Morgan "Monster"
    A-7 Laser Crew Kostas Taliantzis
    A-7 Laser Crew David Beaudoin
    A-7 Laser Crew Black "BR" Eagle
Section Two Leader Cheb "Bacca"
    A-7 Laser Crew Jochen Asel
    A-7 Laser Crew Bruce Curd
    A-7 Laser Crew Clydene Nee
Section Three Leader Dominic Quach
    A-7 Laser Crew James Sasek
    A-7 Laser Crew Justin Cranford
    A-7 Laser Crew Larry Lade

COMPANY HEAVY WEAPONS PLATOON (KORAN PO PAC-4 PARTICLE ACCELERATOR)

Section One Leader Tomas Burgos-Caez
    PAC-4 Crew Mackranack Bajak
    PAC-4 Crew Jonathan Walton
    PAC-4 Crew Ted Hahn
Section Two Leader Tresi Arvizo
    PAC-4 Crew Avi Waksberg
    PAC-4 Crew Michael Atlin
    PAC-4 Crew Tim Franzke

FIRST RIFLE PLATOON (RED HAWKS)

PLATOON HQ TEAM

Platoon Leader Kalen Romano
Platoon Andi Carrison
Messenger Johnathan Wright
Scout with LAS-4K Laser Rifle Raven Brown
Medic Michael Sands

G2 MORTAR TEAM

Leader Luca Beltrami
50mm G2 Mortar Crew Robert Burson
50mm G2 Mortar Crew Porter Williams

SHOCK GROUP A

Group Leader Shane King
    Khuvak Support Laser Crew Ricky Huggs
    Khuvak Support Laser Crew James Kosmicki
    Khuvak Support Laser Crew David Dorward
Shock Trooper Tilde See
Shock Trooper Sara Williamson
Shock Trooper Justin Beeh
Shock Trooper Fuzz "Wuzzy"
Shock Trooper Karl Miller
Shock Trooper Casey Garske

SHOCK GROUP B

Group Leader Jared Sorensen
    Khuvak Support Laser Crew Carl Mccoy
    Khuvak Support Laser Crew Daniel H. Levine
    Khuvak Support Laser Crew Ian McFarlin
Shock Trooper Steve Lord
Shock Trooper Christopher Weuve
Shock Trooper Paul Lantow
Shock Trooper Rawad Sarkis
Shock Trooper Steven "Even"
Shock Trooper Jeremy Cranford

SHOCK GROUP C

Group Leader Luca "Lukos" Carnevale
    Khuvak Support Laser Crew Ahyh "Milahk"
    Khuvak Support Laser Crew Nathan Black
    Khuvak Support Laser Crew Gavran "Snapper"
Shock Trooper Aaron "Wolf Samurai" Roudabush
Shock Trooper Dylan Sara
Shock Trooper Yragael
Shock Trooper Jordan Raymond
Shock Trooper Nolan J Hitchcock
Shock Trooper Chris Pikula

SECOND RIFLE PLATOON (GECKOS)

PLATOON HQ TEAM

Platoon Leader Mark W Roy
Platoon Monte Lin
Messenger Matthew Chin
Scout with LAS-4K Laser Rifle Spice Weasel
Medic Fredrik Holmqvist

G2 MORTAR TEAM

Leader Groot lam
    50mm G2 Mortar Crew Drew South
    50mm G2 Mortar Crew Jack Thomas

SHOCK GROUP A

Group Leader Jon Spengler
    Khuvak Support Laser Crew Viktor Haag
    Khuvak Support Laser Crew Michael Madren
    Khuvak Support Laser Crew Czigány Péter
Shock Trooper Daniel Tavares Moore
Shock Trooper Joe Beason
Shock Trooper Maurice Robinson
Shock Trooper Minneyar "Minotaur"
Shock Trooper Ryan Macklin
Shock Trooper Ross "The Mountain"

SHOCK GROUP B

Group Leader Gunnar Högberg
    Khuvak Support Laser Crew Isaac Karth
    Khuvak Support Laser Crew Herman Duyker
    Khuvak Support Laser Crew Rob Kukuchka
Shock Trooper Jen "General Jen"
Shock Trooper Gary Kacmarcik
Shock Trooper Noah Schoenholtz
Shock Trooper Redat "The Wrecker"
Shock Trooper Verre "Worldbreaker"
Shock Trooper Maliarenko "Bayonet"

CHURCH OF THE TRANSITION

THIRD RIFLE PLATOON (CORD ARCHER)

PLATOON HQ TEAM

Platoon Leader Martijn Waegemakers
Platoon Vaer Saagt
Messenger Dan Grendell
Scout with LAS-4K Laser Rifle Mark Townshend
Medic Jatt Mones

G2 MORTAR TEAM

Leader Eusebi Vazquez
    50mm G2 Mortar Crew Robin Shaw
    50mm G2 Mortar Crew Fredrik Sellevold

SHOCK GROUP A

Group Leader E. Burema
    Khuvak Support Laser Crew Wade Woodson
    Khuvak Support Laser Crew Hlrln
    Khuvak Support Laser Crew Gal Fieri
Shock Trooper Robin Sloan
Shock Trooper Brian "Mac" Smith
Shock Trooper Talassa
Shock Trooper Scott Hill
Shock Trooper Beryl S "Ring"
Shock Trooper Mary Atwell

SHOCK GROUP B

Group Leader Noble "Devastator" Paoletta
    Khuvak Support Laser Crew Kristopher Volter
    Khuvak Support Laser Crew Ron Ursem
    Khuvak Support Laser Crew Kai Nikulainen
Shock Trooper Mark "Mystes" Watson
Shock Trooper Charles Coleman
Shock Trooper Double U
Shock Trooper Andy Agnew
Shock Trooper John Barr
Shock Trooper Glen O'brien

SHOCK GROUP C

Group Leader Erdogyam Khuvak
    Khuvak Support Laser Gurtaj Khuvak
    Khuvak Support Laser Jeffrey Hosmer
    Khuvak Support Laser Crew Rich Warren
Shock Trooper Lukas Myhan
Shock Trooper Petri Wessman
Shock Trooper Matt Gifford
Shock Trooper Jeff Coelho
Shock Trooper Craig "Shaker"
Shock Trooper Jamie Tanner

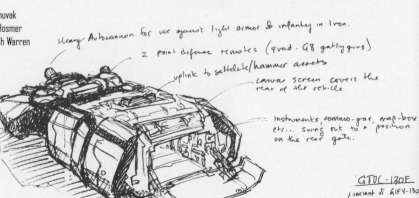

Heavy Autocannon for use against light armor & infantry in Iron.

2 point defense remotes (quad. G8 gatling guns)

uplink to sattelite/hammer assets

Camo screen covers the rear of the vehicle

Instruments, commo-gear, map-box etc... swing out to a position on the rear gate.

GTOC-130E
(variant of GIFV-130
Recrage

GTOC
Tactical Operation's
Center (grav)

CHURCH OF THE TRANSITION

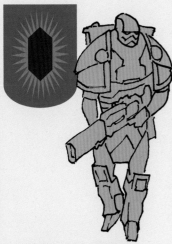

1ST COMPANY, CHURCH OF THE TRANSITION IRON GUARDS REGIMENT, HOTOK

HEADQUARTERS PLATOON

COMPANY HQ TEAM

Company Commander Govneh "Tarkun"
Company Executive Officer Jeremiah Frye
Headquarters Staff Keith Senkowski
Headquarters Staff Good Sport
Medic Cameron Horn
Gunner with SHIS-5A SCrEW Roy RooSack
Gunner with PAC-84i Particle Accelerator
    Ara Hacopian

KORVAL GPTCV INFANTRY FIGHTING VEHICLE SECTION

Vehicle 1 Commander Matt "Catapult" Wang
    Driver Michael Feldhusen
    Gunner Steve Hochberger
    Electronics Link "Hacker"
Vehicle 2 Commander Matthew SB
    Driver Jürgen Mayer
    Gunner Scott "Laser"
    Electronics Dylan Boates
Vehicle 3 Commander Jeremy "Chief"
    Driver Peter Tierney
    Gunner Mark Delsing
    Electronics Mariya Krutova

FIRST PLATOON (BLACK SWORD)

PLATOON HQ TEAM

Platoon Leader Daniel Gonzalez da Costa Campos
Platoon with HIL-4 Laser Rifle Chris "Cutter"
Medic Juan Gomez

IRON GROUP #1

Group Leader Phub Ar
Heavy Weapon Crew with HIL-4 Laser Rifle
    Ed "Blaster"
Iron Trooper Lance
Iron Trooper Rob Hall
Iron Trooper Ken Bo
Iron Trooper Allan Rodda
Iron Trooper Sean Nittner
Iron Trooper Scott Bennett
Iron Trooper Jeff "Torque"

IRON GROUP #2

Group Leader JJ Cano - House of Udulor
Heavy Weapon Crew with HIL-4 Laser Rifle
    Chrno "Mancer"
Iron Trooper John L S Foster
Iron Trooper Tobias "Terror"
Iron Trooper Bill Lucas
Iron Trooper Caley "Omnicool" Rossanova
Iron Trooper Brian Zielinski
Iron Trooper Dan Bailey
Iron Trooper Fan Tomas

IRON GROUP #3

Group Leader Jacob Bean
Heavy Weapon Crew with HIL-4 Laser Rifle
    Justin Akkerman
Iron Trooper Scott Dunphy
Iron Trooper Justin Smith
Iron Trooper Paulo Vicente
Iron Trooper Bill Kelley
Iron Trooper Carl Rigney
Iron Trooper Jeff Brooks
Iron Trooper Chris Messina

SECOND PLATOON (BLACK HAND)

PLATOON HQ TEAM

Platoon Leader Lamp Salesman
Heavy Weapon Crew with HIL-4 Laser Rifle
    Tim "Wizard"
Medic Rich Brassell

IRON GROUP #1

Group Leader Ryan Lasater
Heavy Weapon Crew with HIL-4 Laser Rifle
    Eddie Heywood
Iron Trooper Antonio
Iron Trooper Greg Cooksey
Iron Trooper Jan "The Beast"
Iron Trooper Johnstone Metzger
Iron Trooper Stephen Rider
Iron Trooper Keith "Evil Knight" Mingus
Iron Trooper Colin Jessup

IRON GROUP #2

Group Leader "Fade'em all" Bahl
Heavy Weapon Crew with HIL-4 Laser Rifle
    Sam Zeitlin
Iron Trooper Rick Baer
Iron Trooper Sammo "Whammo"
Iron Trooper Andy Prime
Iron Trooper J Aaron
Iron Trooper Rachel E.S. Walton
Iron Trooper Edward Petersen
Iron Trooper Scott Spieker

IRON GROUP #3

Group Leader Scott Peacock
Heavy Weapon Crew with HIL-4 Laser Rifle Silas "The Monk"
Iron Trooper Devin Night
Iron Trooper Gary M "Shambler"
Iron Trooper Jonathan M. White
Iron Trooper AJ "Jackmaster"
Iron Trooper Adam Schwaninger
Iron Trooper Grumpy Face
Iron Trooper Michael Meltzer

THIRD PLATOON (BLACK FLAME)

PLATOON HQ TEAM

Platoon Leader Wolfgang Müller
Heavy Weapon Crew with HIL-4 Laser Rifle
    Tom Lynch
Medic Doctor Kreuz

IRON GROUP #1

Group Leader Steve "Giggles" Prescott
Heavy Weapon Crew with HIL-4 Laser Rifle
    Evelyn Tromp
Iron Trooper Glen "Hunter"
Iron Trooper Ryan Garcia
Iron Trooper D'lait "Eagle"
Iron Trooper Dennis Wiedbusch
Iron Trooper Jeff "Boomer"
Iron Trooper Genghis Dempsey
Iron Trooper Matt Richardson

IRON GROUP #2

Group Leader Clyde L. Rhoer the 3rd
Heavy Weapon Crew with HIL-4 Laser Rifle
    Chris "Red" McLaren
Iron Trooper Thane "SCLP" Avers
Iron Trooper Brian Thibeault
Iron Trooper Mayuran Tiruchelvam
Iron Trooper John Mehrholz
Iron Trooper Gregg Anderson
Iron Trooper David Cornwell
Iron Trooper Aram "Wrangler"